Thunderfoot

Mel moved forward cautiously. There was a sudden noise, as if someone was loudly blowing his nose. Her heart was beating wildly. Before she had time to turn and flee, a huge white shape loomed up before her. Blowing through its nostrils like a lorry with a broken exhaust was the largest horse Mel had ever seen. He was nearly the height of a shire horse, but more massively built. His enormous hooves were the size of lampshades, his legs like knotted tree trunks.

To my parents, Gwen and Derek Kartun

Thunderfoot

Deborah
van der Beek

Scholastic Children's Books,
Scholastic Publications Ltd,
7–9 Pratt Street, London NW1 0AE, UK

Scholastic Inc.,
555 Broadway, New York, NY 10012-3999, USA

Scholastic Canada Ltd,
123 Newkirk Road, Richmond Hill,
Ontario, Canada L4C 3G5

Ashton Scholastic Pty Ltd,
P O Box 579, Gosford, New South Wales,
Australia

Ashton Scholastic Ltd,
Private Bag 92801, Penrose, Auckland,
New Zealand

First published by Scholastic Children's Books, 1994

ISBN 0 590 55814 5

Typeset by TW Typesetting, Midsomer Norton, Avon
Printed by Cox & Wyman Ltd, Reading, Berks.

10 9 8 7 6 5 4 3

Chapter 1

Mel turned the corner of the grimy street they lived in and headed up the next at a jog-trot. Past the chicken processing factory (which her brother, Davy, always refused to go anywhere near) and along Signal Lane. Everywhere she went people waved or "hulloed" to her. Even in a medium-sized town the size of Oxley, everyone knew Melany Whitby the milkman's daughter.

At the top of the hill she paused to catch her breath, and looked at the town spread beneath her, ending sharply along the line of the railway. She could see the dairy, where her father worked, and next to it the only field on the town side. More or less square, the field consisted of rough grass and brambles. There were a few trees, and an animal shelter in an advanced state of ruin.

It was here that Mel was heading. Now almost wrapped in bramble and wild clematis, the shed had been discovered by the family when Mel was quite small.

She couldn't put a number on the many picnics and games she and Davy had played there over the years. These days she simply used it as a quiet place to read or – as now – do homework.

Mel squeezed under the fence and stopped dead. Something was wrong. A large post which partly supported the shed roof had been knocked clean away and the roof was sagging badly. Vandals! Mel moved forward cautiously. There was a sudden noise, as if someone was loudly blowing his nose. Her heart was beating wildly. Before she had time to turn and flee, a huge white shape loomed up before her. Blowing through its nostrils like a lorry with a broken exhaust was the largest horse Mel had ever seen. He was nearly the height of a shire horse, but more massively built. His enormous hooves were the size of lampshades, his legs like knotted tree trunks. He was also extremely ugly.

The horse moved one step nearer. Mel could feel the ground beneath her tremble. "Hello, you," she said.

Encouraged by the sound of her voice, the animal moved forward again, and dropping its nose, gently sniffed her hand. Mel could have been frightened, but wasn't – the animal simply oozed friendliness; he was so obviously glad to see her. Mel stroked his neck, noticing as she did so the dirt matting his mane and coat, and the way his ribs stuck out, like the wreck of an abandoned ship. "Sorry, old boy," she apologized, "I haven't even got a biscuit for you."

How odd that he should just appear like this. No one had ever used this field for animals before: Mel had always imagined that it was just a bit of wasteland. Thinking more carefully, she realized that it probably belonged to the farm on the other side of the railway. And whoever owned that must own the horse.

So why wasn't that somebody looking after him?

Mel looked across the field to the gate. Beyond it was a track leading through a tunnel under the railway embankment, to the farmhouse. She walked over. In the tunnel was another gate, a high one. There were rolls of barbed wire at the top and, as usual, the gate was padlocked. She peered through. Just a corner of the house was visible at some distance, but little else.

Apart from the tunnel, the only way you could reach the house was over a bridge two or three miles beyond the town.

Perhaps I ought to go there and find out, Mel

thought. Maybe the horse's owner didn't know he was hungry. Somehow, she doubted it.

She patted the horse goodbye, and he stood watching her up the road. At the top she looked round; he was still there. She gave a wave and turned for home.

Chapter 2

"Ouch! It's hot. But it's absolutely delicious. Here, take your head out of that horse book for a moment and tell me."

Mel took the saucepan and dipped a cautious finger into warm, chocolatey gunge.

"Umm! It's brilliant, Mum!" The finger went in again. Davy's head popped up from the complicated construction he was glueing together. "I want some!"

"I want doesn't get", Mrs Whitby was about to say.

"Please!" added Davy shrilly, following Mel,

who had nipped under the table and round the back of a chair.

"Superman to the rescue," he cried. "Wicked Pig-woman has stolen the wonderful elixir of – of—"

"Immortality?" suggested Mum, swooping to catch the teapot, which had somehow been knocked flying. "And Mel, do let Davy have a taste before anything gets broken." Mel reluctantly handed over the pan.

"Just one taste, mind, or there won't be enough for Dad's cake. And please give Alice the spoon to lick – make sure it's cool enough." Alice, whose fat little legs were pumping up and down in delight stretched out a plump hand from the high chair. Mel took a last, wistful sniff and gave it into her sister's expectant grasp. They all watched as Alice turned the spoon over and over suspiciously. She banged it on the table so that chocolate spattered everywhere. Alice liked that, and did it again. This time a bit landed on her mouth. Suddenly, an electric thrill ran through her. She froze, and there came onto her face a look of utmost surprise and pleasure. Was this stuff really true? After that, every morsel was polished off most efficiently.

"More?" said Alice hopefully.

But Mrs Whitby had taken the pan and was pouring warm chocolate over a large cake, smoothing and spreading it with a palette-knife.

"I only wish Alice felt that way about lunch. You should have seen the disgusting mess she made this morning. Flung it everywhere."

"Oh!" asked Davy eagerly. "Did you save any for Dot?" Dot was Davy's pet hen. She was huge and bad tempered, and pecked everyone except Davy, but she had a proud red comb, and a beautiful green sheen on her black feathers. Davy adored her and very much wanted to keep more hens, but their garden was small, so Mr and Mrs Whitby wouldn't let him. Dot did have her uses though: her eggs were in the cake.

“Four days’ worth in one go!” breathed Davy, looking at it admiringly.

But then it wasn’t every day your father had his forty-fifth birthday, was it?

At that moment, there was the slight noise of a key turning in the lock.

“Dad?” said Mel, puzzled. “He shouldn’t be home yet.” Then, “It’s Dad!! Hide the cake!”

But Mr Whitby seemed to be taking his time. Davy went back to his construction, Mel to her book. Mrs Whitby looked at the bowed heads fondly. Mel and Davy small and dark like herself, Alice like their father, broad and fair. She glanced at the title of Mel’s book: *You and Your Horse.* Another book, *A Pony for Kate*, lay beside her on the table.

Both Mrs Whitby’s older children were passionate about animals. She would have loved to own a grassy orchard so Davy could keep chickens and to give Mel regular riding lessons. It simply wasn’t possible on a milkman’s wages.

And she couldn't really go back to teaching yet, not with Alice so small . . .

"Hello, Sam."

Mr Whitby came into the room. Mel gave up pretending to read her book and smiled up at him.

"Hello, Da—" she began, and stopped abruptly. Mr Whitby's face was quite grey and stiff; his huge frame moved more slowly than usual. He dropped heavily into a chair, and just sat there, not looking at them, saying nothing.

Mrs Whitby had also realized that something was up.

"Sam," she said. "What's happened?"

With a horrible lurch of the stomach, Mel realized – was it possible that her father was going to cry? What could be wrong? What could be so bad that her big, strong father was on the verge of tears? You expected children to cry, and Mum always wept (though she pretended she wasn't) during the soppy bits of films. This was different though: this was real.

She willed him not to. She willed him as hard as she could, until it almost hurt. Davy's eyes were as round as a robin's.

They all waited. Gradually Dad's breathing eased.

After a long time, he ran an enormous hand through his gingery hair, and said, "I suppose I'd better begin at the beginning."

The kettle hummed, and Dad's voice rumbled round the room like a winter bumble-bee on a cold sunny day.

The dairy Mr Whitby worked for was called Fosset and Sons Dairy Limited, which was a long name for a very small firm. The word "Sons" wasn't even correct, as old Mr Fosset didn't have any, only one daughter who had gone to live in Canada. The name referred to Mr Fosset himself, and his father, the Fosset of the title.

Lately, things had not been going too well for the firm. Three of the four milk floats were on their last legs. Several times one had broken down in the middle of a round. Lots of people had become fed up with this, and had cancelled their orders.

"I'd offer to mend the things myself," Mr Whitby said, "but . . . as you know, I'm er . . . not too good with machines."

They did know. They all smiled, remembering ancient cars that broke down as soon as they drove off on holiday, hoovers that blew instead of sucked.

"I liked the exploding toaster best, Dad. That was brilliant," said Davy.

Dad gave Alice, who had been released from her high chair and had crawled into his lap, a little squeeze, and carried on.

"Yesterday, just as I was leaving on my first round, a man came into the office. He was smartly dressed in a smooth sort of way, and had a flash new car. But something about the way he moved, and his sniffing around, reminded me of a pig: the sort that is just waiting for the farmer to make one false move, and it'll have his leg off. I thought he was a new customer. And heaven knows we need them, pig-eyed or not!

"When I came back for a new load of milk, Mr Fosset asked to speak to me. He looked . . ." Dad searched for what had made him think something might be up. "Well, no, he didn't look at me. That was what was odd. Mr Fosset told me that the man I had seen was a chap called Bullhead – a Mr Marshall Bullhead. He owns the Freshco Supermarkets – there's one in town."

Mel nodded. She remembered Freshco in the High Street: a big shiny place, with large signs in luminous yellow. It was always being advertised on the local radio.

"Anyway, Freshco want to expand their dairy side of things, and having someone doing a doorstep service in the area was 'a bit of a nuisance', according to Mr Bullhead."

Mr Whitby took the cup of tea Mum pushed towards him, and carried on. "Mr Bullhead made Ted Fosset an offer to buy his house and the dairy in one."

"Buy the dairy!" Mum said.

"And the house!" Mel added. "He must be loaded."

"He is." Mr Whitby gave a wry grin. "And it was a rotten offer, too."

"Mr Fosset didn't accept, then?" Mum said.

"Well, a while back Ted Fosset told me about his retirement plans. He and his wife were finding that big house they live in a bit much, and with the milk round not doing too well, the garden was going to rack and ruin. He told me how much he hates seeing it like that. In a few years' time they had thought they might sell out and move to a small cottage by the sea – he's got an interest in budgerigars. He wants to spend more time breeding them."

"What kind of budgerigars?" Davy asked. But Mr Whitby didn't know.

"So Ted Fosset has agreed to sell," he continued.

"But why, if it was such a bad offer?" Mum asked.

"Cash," said Dad. "The offer means an immediate payment, as soon as the Fossets move out. They've seen a cottage they like the look of and so . . . It was too tempting to refuse, and a quick way out of his business troubles too."

Holding the mug of tea in both hands, he blew on it, frowning. "I've been working for Fosset for nearly ten years . . . Although I knew things weren't going well, I always thought we'd pull through somehow. This was something I had just not expected."

"Oh dear," Mum said. "Bullhead doesn't sound nearly such a nice man to work for."

Mr Whitby looked at her sharply. "Oh, no," he said. "That's not it at all. Mr Bullhead doesn't want to run the dairy himself. I expect he wants to do up Mr Fosset's house and sell it or something. But the dairy – that'll just close."

For a long moment they all stared at him, and the only sound in the kitchen was a constant soft murmur from Alice. It was Dad who broke it.

"So," he ended up. "So . . . I've lost my job."

Only Mrs Whitby understood exactly what this might mean; how bad things would become. For Mel and Davy, there was rather a feeling of "so what?"

"Can't you just get another job?" Davy asked.

"That's not so easy these days," Mum said.

"Not in this town," said Dad. "And then . . . there's something else."

Mel watched. The wooden look had come back into his eyes. She wanted to hug him, but she was afraid of making him upset again. Instead, she just crept nearer and leaned up against his leg. Dad looked down, pulled gently at a lock of her hair and carried on.

"I've always got on with Ted Fosset – until now – and I've been working there a long time. Longer than anyone else. I knew he was near retirement age, and he often talked about the little cottage he planned to buy."

"And the budgies," said Davy.

"And the budgies . . . and . . . maybe I was silly . . . but, well, I had hoped he'd retire, but keep me on as manager. It was such a shock to hear of him selling up altogether."

"You weren't silly at all," said Mel stoutly. "You'd make a jolly good manager."

"I know I would," said Dad with a trace of his former self.

"It's Mr Fosset that's silly," cried Davy. "Silly old pilly old stupid Mr Fosset. I hate him." His lip wobbled. "I'm going out to feed Dot."

"I'm going out, too," Mel said.

"Next door?" asked Mum. But Mel shook her head. She didn't feel like telling even Angeline yet. She wanted to be alone. She needed to think, to try and make sense of what had just happened. Probably Mum and Dad would like to be alone, too.

"Railway field," Mel said. She had already told her mother about the mysterious horse she had found there.

"Here. I've got an old carrot or two," Mrs Whitby said. "Take them."

Mel remembered that Davy kept a sack of flaked corn in the shed for Dot. Surely the horse would like some of that too? She could take it in a plastic bag. Mel was just about to ask her mother, when she suddenly realized that perhaps she shouldn't. Now Dad was losing his job they would have to watch every penny – and the amount of corn a horse could eat would be expensive. She rushed upstairs to where she kept her birthday savings. There was a fair bit: she had had a birthday quite recently. "I want to help," she said to Dad, holding it out to him.

But to her surprise, Mr Whitby's face clouded over. He looked almost angry. "No!" he said in a tight voice, and turned away. Then, more gently, he added, "Thanks all the same. I couldn't take your birthday money."

"Don't worry," Mrs Whitby said. "I'm sure we'll be all right."

As Mel clicked the front gate after her she noticed a face at an upstairs window next door: Angeline. But Mel looked away and carried on up the road.

Mel sat in the tumbledown animal shelter. The horse stood in the doorway and looked down at her in a friendly way. She could feel the warmth of his grassy breath, and it comforted her.

What did losing your job really mean? How would it affect them all? She'd felt so helpless with Dad – just a child, not understanding, unable to help.

"At least I can help you in a small way," she told the horse. "You liked those carrots, didn't you?" The animal made a sort of "whuffing" noise through his nose. "That means yes," she said.

Suddenly Mel thought of one very good reason why he was so thin: perhaps the owner had only just bought him – from a wicked

dealer – like you read about in books. Then she had another thought. Maybe there were lots of other horses too, on the other side of the railway . . . a new livery stables or something. If that were true, then they might need people to help look after them. Could she get a Saturday job there? She began to feel excited at the very thought. And if it were a proper job, then surely Mum and Dad wouldn't mind taking money from her? How pleased they would be. Mel pictured their happy faces as she handed over a fat wad of cash. She felt more grown up, more useful at once. Why had she not thought of it before?

I knew coming here would help. It always does, she thought.

"I've got to go now," she told the horse, "because it's Dad's birthday tea. But tomorrow I'll go and find out all about you . . . and see if there is a job for me. I'll go as soon as school is over."

School. Now there was a thought. What

would everyone at school make of Dad losing his job?

Chapter 3

The next day was rainy. Mel pulled on her school coat and shivered.

Yesterday's birthday tea hadn't been as bad as she'd feared. Alice's wild enthusiasm when she saw the cake again had cheered them all up. And though they had said Mel was a bit young, and it wasn't necessary, Mum and Dad had been pleased and touched when she declared her intention to find a Saturday job.

Today, however, things looked grey again. She dreaded telling her classmates. It would be so embarrassing. Then she felt ashamed at being ashamed: it wasn't Dad's fault. But she guessed how much people would gossip behind her back. She hated the thought of them pitying her.

Her thoughts were broken by the sound of racing footsteps, and a panting Angeline caught her up. Plump Angeline was not built for running. She had several books under one arm and a bulging plastic bag and a folder under the other. Her hair had been hastily pulled back into a pony-tail and was in a mess. Angeline hated her long, reddish hair, and was always threatening to cut it off, but her parents wouldn't let her.

"Mum told me this morning I'm not ladylike enough – well, tough!" Angeline asserted, wiping her nose on her sleeve in a distinctly unladylike manner.

Despite herself, Mel smiled. Poor Angeline's parents! They gave their daughter a name like that, hoping she'd be sweet and good. With the Angeline Mel knew, they were on to a loser.

Angeline continued. "I saw you last night. I knew something was wrong."

In a flat, sullen voice, Mel told her the whole story. Angeline's lumpy face was dark with sympathy. "Hang on a minute." She stopped and fiddled around, trying to stuff her folder into the plastic bag. It was obviously a hopeless task. Mel took it from her. Angeline slipped her now free arm through Mel's. "Come on," she said. "We'll go in together."

Mel found herself the reluctant member of a clan she had not known about before: the clan of the unemployed. They were bound together by something all of them felt, but none of them could quite explain. They didn't speak about it much, but when they did it was in private huddles, with sidelong glances lest anyone else should be listening. The other children politely pretended not to notice.

Why are we behaving as if we are ashamed? Mel wondered. Perhaps it was something to do with pride. She remembered how proud she had been when Dad had won the father's race at sports day. Angeline's father had been last, and Angeline had covered her face with her hands and squealed in embarrassment. Losing your job was like losing a race, only much more serious.

And it was Mr Fosset's fault that the dairy was closing, not Dad's. She knew that even if everyone else didn't.

The day was even worse than she had expected, and without Angeline's cheery loudness, she would have found it hard to bear.

Only the thought of going to the farm and of seeing the horse again raised her spirits slightly. That day school seemed endless.

Then at last the bell rang and it was time to go home. Waiting at the bus stop, Mel felt cold. She'd just missed a bus, and her coat was still wet from the morning. Stamping her feet to keep warm, she wandered over to the nearest shop, and idly looked in through the window.

It was a pet shop. Mel remembered that they were almost out of cat food at home. She went in and asked for the brand favoured by the family cat, Baldrick. While the woman went off to fetch a tin, Mel looked about her. In one corner of a glass cabinet, covered in dust, was a set of brushes which she knew from her books were used on horses. If she got a job with horses, she'd certainly need to buy some of those and in that way she could still use her birthday money to help Dad. She twisted her head around, trying to see the prices, but eventually asked.

"Those brushes have been sitting there for years," said the shop assistant, taking them out. "Look, they're still at the old, cheap price."

"Could you possibly keep them for me? Just till tomorrow?" Mel asked. She could scarcely keep the excitement from her voice. "I – I'll know by then whether I've got a job in some stables."

"Of course," the woman said. "We used to

sell a lot of these brushes, way back. This was where people used to pick up the bus for the old riding stables, you know, by the railway."

"Was it by the tunnel?" Mel asked, with some interest.

"That's right. It's closed down now . . . like everything decent round here. Still, I expect you're too young to remember that." The woman rambled on about how things used to be. Mel, disappointed, listened with increasing impatience.

"Please, who owns the stables now?"

"Oh, some dealer bloke. He buys and sells farm stock and things. Machinery, animals – anything."

"Horses?" breathed Mel. Maybe there was still a job in it for her?

"Cattle mostly, I think. Fatstock? Horses? I don't know. Maybe." The woman looked uncomfortable. "He's not the type of fellow I'd care to pass the time of day with."

Mel thanked the woman and left the shop.

So the place belonged to a dealer: someone not altogether pleasant either. Should she not bother to go at all? It didn't sound like the job she had hoped for. But she owed it to Mum and Dad – and to the horse – to at least try. However, she began to dread the expedition.

The farm track did not look promising. It was overgrown with brambles, and dotted with bits of rusting machinery. Once or twice Mel slipped into a rut, and her inadequate school shoes filled with rainwater. Over and over, she rehearsed what she would say to the man, and each time it seemed more difficult. What could you say? "Please sir, I would like a job with animals, and by the way, what is that starving horse doing in your field?" He'd probably laugh in her face. Or more likely be angry. What had the woman in the pet shop meant? Would the man get violent? By the time Mel had entered the farmyard, her heart was beating so hard it felt as though it might fly from her chest.

The farmhouse was of ancient red brick, far smaller than she had expected and surrounded by stables and outbuildings of all shapes and sizes.

It must have looked lovely as a riding stables, Mel thought, imagining horses' heads looking over the stable doors, others standing being groomed, and the sound of hooves. But now she saw and heard nothing. Where were all the animals?

She set her teeth, and with an air of determination, strode up to the door and knocked hard.

The sound echoed eerily round the yard. Mel waited. Nothing. After some time, she gained enough courage to peer through the letterbox. A sharp smell of damp, and of something else, something slightly unpleasant, hit her. She looked in. The house was completely empty. No furniture. Nothing.

She was about to move away, when a sudden movement behind a window caught her eye.

Mel froze in terror. The two eyes blinked, then disappeared. A minute later, a small face appeared at the window. "Miaow!" it said plaintively.

"Poor puss!" cried Mel. "Are you shut in?" But she should have known better. The little cat, black all over save for a white splash on its nose, jumped through a broken pane, and began to twine itself about her feet.

"You terrified me, little Spook," Mel scolded, bending down to stroke the animal. It could only have been young, but already it was heavily pregnant. It was terribly thin. "Where will you have your kittens?" Mel asked. "Inside the house, I suppose."

What good luck I bought some cat food, she thought. Baldrick could wait for once – he was already disgustingly fat and lazy. The little cat could scarcely wait, and hopped from paw to paw, mewing anxiously.

But although Mel tried hard, scraping her fingers badly on a stone, she could not open the tin. It was infuriating. Eventually, feeling very guilty, Mel gave up. She would just have to come tomorrow with a tin-opener.

It had been rather an unsuccessful journey. She had met no one and found out little. Something white on the back of a swinging door caught her eye. It was a notice. Mel read it.

"FOR SALE. Farmhouse and outbuildings plus 72 acres of good grazing land. Apply . . ." So the place was for sale! Mel felt disappointment surge through her. People might leave a cat – on a farm, cats were hardly noticed – but they wouldn't leave a horse . . . He'd probably be gone already. She ran towards the railway tunncl to scc if she could catch a glimpse of him. She pressed her face against the gate, but not much of the field was visible. She could have cried with frustration. She would have to go all the way round by bus. But rattling the padlock, it suddenly gave way in her hands. The gate had been unlocked. Without stopping to wonder why or who had unlocked it, she pushed through.

She was in the field in seconds. And there he was. She was so pleased to see him, she shouted out and waved. The horse lifted his great head and blew a welcome through hairy nostrils.

"Here, boy!" she cried. And the horse came at a lumbering canter. The ground shook beneath his gigantic hooves.

"Blimey!" breathed Mel. "That must be at least five on the Richter scale!

"I'll have to give you a name, you know. Jumbo?" Mel reflected. Too undignified. Titan? Maximus? Thunderfoot? Thunderfoot. Yes, that should do.

"That's what I'll call you," she told him. "Thunderfoot."

But I shouldn't be doing this! she thought. I mustn't get too fond of him – he could be taken away at any time. Thunderfoot dropped velvet lips into Mel's hand, and fumbled gently. It was too late.

Chapter 4

Mr Whitby still had several weeks to work before the dairy closed down. After that, what? Of course he'd look for work elsewhere; but how likely was he to get it?

At school, it was much discussed amongst the "clan".

"My dad just watches telly all day now," said one girl. "Lucky devil!" But Mel knew she was just trying to make the best of it.

Had none of the fathers found other work? Would Mel's father be the same?

"Yes, they get like that," said another. "They

try really hard at first – my dad wrote millions of letters, went to loads of interviews. Did he get anything? Huh! No!"

My father won't be like theirs, thought Mel. He'll keep trying. He'll find something. But then you always thought your own parents were safe from knocks, didn't you? It was that pride again. It was a shock to feel a cold wind blowing through the protective family wall.

Nothing had exactly changed yet; maybe it wouldn't. Maybe Dad would find a new job easily, and Mel wouldn't have to take out full membership of this group of children with neatly darned clothes that didn't quite fit any more. She'd started noticing things like that – and she knew she'd hate it as much as they did. It was just something she was going to have to get used to. A chill dread rose in Mel's heart. It seemed as if her safe, golden childhood was suddenly at an end, with the real world battering to get in.

Over and over again Mel cursed Mr Fosset. It

was all due to him that they were in this mess! If only he'd asked Dad to be his partner, everything might have been all right – because Dad would never have asked himself. Sometimes perhaps you needed to be a bit pushy, and Dad wasn't like that. A gentle giant . . . rather like old Thunderfoot, thought Mel. She couldn't stop thinking about the horse, counting the hours at school till she could run off and see if he was still there. Even if she didn't know who owned him yet, whoever did could only be pleased if she fed him, looked after him a bit. And there was the little cat too. Mel felt the glow of her own goodness. She felt better at once.

The woman in the pet shop broke into a smile. "You got the job then?"

"Er, well, not exactly but I . . ." Mel felt the tin-opener in her pocket. "I came in for some more cat food, actually."

"Don't you want the grooming stuff then?"

Mel looked wistfully at the brushes. It would be lovely to have them, but unless she had a job there was no excuse to buy luxuries. "What would I need?" she asked hesitantly.

"Not done it before then?"

Mel shook her head. The woman began pulling things out of the display cabinet.

"Right then. You begin with the dandy, then the body – circular strokes like this . . . cleaning the brush like this with the curry . . ." All these names she had read about for so long – there they all were! Mel listened, entranced, almost with her mouth watering. It was no good. She had to have those brushes if it took every single bit of saved money . . . and as the woman had said, she *was* getting them very cheap.

The horse was in the middle of the field when Mel arrived, pulling in a half-hearted way at a clump of coarse grass. But it was the hungry cat who needed attention first. Mel took the tin out of her bag and walked over to the railway

tunnel. She rattled the gate, but it had been locked again. Who by? she wondered vaguely. She would have to leave the food by the gate. She spooned some cat food into a saucer she had brought, and the little cat appeared as if by magic. It fell upon the food like a dog, gulping down great mouthfuls ravenously. Golden eyes flashed "thank you", and the little cat disappeared towards the farmhouse once more.

Mel watched her go and then turned back to the horse. As she climbed into the field with him, he caught sight of her and lumbered over.

"I'm going to groom you today," she told him. "Only I haven't done it before, so you will have to be very good."

The horse snorted, and gently butted her with his nose. Mel couldn't decide whether this meant he approved or not. Nervously, she picked up the dandy brush, and began to get the mud from his coat. But her first strokes were too timid. Thunderfoot threw up his head and shuddered, for she was tickling him horribly. Mel leapt back in a fright.

Realizing the problem, she brushed harder. After the dandy, the body brush. Now she was really beginning to get the hang of it. There was only one problem: unless Thunderfoot stood next to a convenient tree-stump, she couldn't reach up very high. Also, he could simply walk off and leave her standing there!

"I shall have to make you a halter, so I can tie you up," she told him.

But at this moment Thunderfoot was not going anywhere – he was enjoying being groomed after so long. Mel's arm moved in rhythmical, circular motions, getting out all the nasty, itchy dirt. It was astonishing how much flew out! Thunderfoot leaned into her arm. His eyelids drooped, and he let out a little grunt of pleasure. "Shove over!" she scolded him. "You're too heavy to lean on me like that."

The horse grunted, and shifted himself reluctantly.

When she reckoned she had finished, Mel stood back. She saw a different animal. Now she could see the soft dappling on his flanks, the darker points, and the flowing white mane and tail. She put away her tools with real pride.

Thunderfoot was still in a sort of trance. "You may be clean," she told him, "but you look like an old grandad." Perhaps he *is* old? she thought. You told a horse's age by looking at its teeth. Mel sat on the fence and flicked through the pages of her library book. (Why was it that library books were always due back when you most needed them? she wondered.) Holding it open at the right page, with the other hand, she timidly parted his lips. Thunderfoot appeared surprised, but did not object.

It was rather puzzling. According to the book, he was either very old or very young. Mel could not decide which. She shut the book crossly.

* * *

Later, in the library to renew the book, Mel saw a notice pinned to the wall. "Starting a small business? Contact the Enterprise Allowance Scheme."

It would be good if Dad could start up his own business, Mel thought. But doing what? Anyway, you must need lots of money to do that. And money was something that was going to be in short supply from now on. Mel dismissed the idea from her mind, and went home.

From then on, Mel visited Thunderfoot every day. Each time she reached the top of the hill overlooking his field, her heart was in her mouth. Would he be there? But he always was.

After a week or so he recognized her from quite a way off, and came over to wait for her.

Once he didn't. Mel saw a small group of children standing at the far gate, chatting to him and patting him. She felt a pang of jealousy. But she needn't have worried. Thunderfoot turned round as soon as she saw her and gallumphed over.

"Isn't he lovely? Isn't he big!" said the children. "Is he yours?"

Mel, though wishing very much to pretend ownership, had to admit he was not.

The children ran off.

Mel had not tried very hard to find out who the horse belonged to. Nor had she made any effort to look for another job. The truth was, she had an uncomfortable feeling that, if found, the horse's owner might ask her to keep away. A job would also keep her from seeing him. And Mel had become so attached to Thunderfoot that she resented any time spent away from him.

Chapter 5

Mr Whitby was dressing up to go out for a job interview.

"How do I look?" he asked Mel.

"Er . . ." Mel didn't want to be rude. The trouble was, a suit and tie never looked right on Dad – he sort of bulged in all the wrong places. The jacket was too tight across the shoulders, and pulled up under the arms in wrinkles. Also, the sleeves were too short.

"You look funny," said Davy.

Eventually, Mum found a smartish jumper that didn't look too bad instead.

"But I hate this jumper," Dad grumbled.

"That's probably why it's the only one without holes in," said Mum. "So you'll have to wear it."

"What job is it anyway?" Mel asked.

"It's in a toy-making workshop," Dad told her. "Could be quite good. I'm not bad at woodwork."

"Won't there be lots of machines?" Davy asked, his mind already working on the glorious possibilities of toys that had got all mixed up: trains with legs, dolls with flashing-siren eyes.

"Well, I'm going to have a go anyway," Mr Whitby said.

But Davy was right. The "workshop" turned out to be more of a factory; the toys mostly plastic.

"Not much of a place to work," Dad told them on his return. "I didn't get the job anyway." Despite the cheerful tone of voice, Mel felt Dad was trying hard to hide his disappointment: after all, it was his first failure.

Was it the first of many? Mel wondered.

That evening, Mr and Mrs Whitby scoured the job section of the local paper.

"What about this one, Sam? 'Pretty, well turned out assistant needed for smart florist shop, apply Rosie's Posies'!"

They laughed. But then Mum became serious. "There's nothing here, Sam. Nothing you'd really like doing."

"I know," Dad rubbed his rough chin thoughtfully. "I've always enjoyed my job. Always – until now – got on with Mr Fosset. Lots of people do jobs they don't enjoy. You have to if you've got responsibilities."

Responsibilities? He means us – me! Mel thought.

She began to realize what it might all mean, Dad being unemployed. The more she thought about it, the less she liked it. Mel looked down at her trousers. There was a thin patch on the knee. Mel hated sewing. Already too, she had noticed changes in the food they ate: stew, instead of the usual roast beef on Sundays, and rather more potatoes. Mel had said nothing, and had avoided her mother's eye. Mrs Whitby knew Mel wasn't fond of stew, and was grateful for her daughter's silence.

Suddenly Mel was angry: angry with Mr Fosset, angry at not being able to ask for new clothes, and angry too at her own helplessness. She hated everyone at school knowing Dad was out of work, hated being branded one of the "clan", with parents who had "failed" to provide for their children. She knew that that was what people thought, although they were too polite (or cowardly) to say so. Worse, she hated the feeling of guilt every time she remembered her own half-hearted attempt to find a Saturday job. I really must try again, she thought . . .

"Don't let's worry too much," said Mum comfortingly. "There's nothing in the paper today, but maybe tomorrow . . . We've twelve weeks yet."

This was both true, and not true. Mr Fosset had had to give his men twelve weeks' notice before the job actually finished. The trouble was, several weeks had already gone by . . .

Mel threw herself into looking after Thunderfoot.

She had made him a halter from some of Dad's rope. The first time she put it on, he flung his head about wildly, trying to shake it off. Perhaps I've made it too tight? she worried. Was something hurting him? After a bit, however, he calmed down, and forgot about it.

Now she could tie him up, grooming became much easier.

Getting Thunderfoot to the right place to groom him was harder. He did not seem to understand what she wanted when she tried to lead him.

Maybe because I'm so small compared to him, he simply doesn't take any notice of me, she thought. However, with the aid of a few cabbage leaves held in front of his nose, he eventually got the idea.

Mel realized it would be useful if she could get the horse to respond to her word, rather than feebly tugging at a rein.

"Wa-alk!" she would say, and praise and pat him if he did so. She talked to him a lot, and after a bit she could see his ears straining towards her, listening. She used up an awful lot of old cabbage leaves these days. Sometimes she treated him to some of Davy's flaked corn which he wolfed down. But although clean and cared for now, Thunderfoot was as thin as ever. Mel knew he needed something more, but corn was expensive, and she could only buy a little occasionally. What good was only a little corn to a horse Thunderfoot's size?

Spook the cat had had her kittens and Mel

had to buy food for her, too. It was all getting to be more than she could afford. She couldn't ask Mum for extra either.

Vaguely, Mel realized that soon she would have to do something. But what? And who should she go to? The RSPCA? Suppose they took Thunderfoot away? Mel walked round the outside of the field and pulled out armfuls of long grass: there didn't seem to be much left in his field. She pushed the problem from her mind. There was something else too . . . his hooves needed trimming, badly.

One day, Angeline came to see Thunderfoot.

"That's no horse, that's a bloomin' dinosaur," she pronounced.

Mel showed off what she had taught him. "Walk on," she said, and "Who-a!" Thunderfoot responded beautifully, and Mel didn't even have to tug on the halter – not once. She had never tried to go above a walk. Somehow, the idea of several tons of horse gallumphing dangerously near her size threes worried even Mel.

Angeline always said she didn't like horses, but was nevertheless impressed.

"Have you tried riding him?"

"I don't know," Mel began doubtfully. "I mean he doesn't belong to me . . ."

"Has anyone been near him?" demanded Angeline.

"No," Mel confessed.

"Go on then," Angeline dared.

"But I can't ride properly," Mel protested.

"You couldn't groom, could you? Or do anything with a horse before? Anyway, I'm not asking you to ride in the Olympics, just sit on his back. Come on, I'll hold him." Angeline took hold of the rein. "Ugh! He's not going to dribble all over me, is he? Yuk! You horrible animal." Mel grinned to see Angeline wiping her hands with a grubby handkerchief.

Mel stood on the tree-stump, and pressed her hands on Thunderfoot's broad back. His

ears swivelled back, but he did not move. She vaulted on.

It was wonderful. She felt incredibly high up, but Thunderfoot was so wide, she felt quite safe. "I can see for miles!" she told Angeline.

Thunderfoot craned his neck round to look at her. "What is this peculiar creature going to get up to next?" he seemed to be saying. All at once Angeline collapsed into giggles, laughing and laughing until she could hardly stand.

"If only you could see how funny you look," she screeched. "You're so small – and he's so big. You look like a robin on an – iceberg!" and Angeline fell into fresh cackles.

Mel blushed furiously. It had taken a lot of guts to get up there. It wasn't her fault she was so small.

Suddenly, without warning, Thunderfoot let out the most enormous neigh. Angeline gave a squawk like a frightened chicken, and was the other side of the fence in a flash. Now it was Mel's turn to laugh.

After that, Mel often got on Thunderfoot's back. It wasn't like real riding, of course, but then she had hardly ever ridden before; to her it was marvellous. And there are some advantages to riding without a saddle. Perhaps it was because she now knew Thunderfoot so well too, but Mel imagined she felt his every thought through the warm ribcage.

If it hadn't been for Dad losing his job, Mel would have been gloriously happy. She stuck out her tongue in the direction of Fosset's Dairy, half hoping someone might see her.

Mel was coming dangerously near to forgetting Thunderfoot did not belong to her . . .

Chapter 6

Mel was on her way to see Thunderfoot. Eleven weeks had gone by; just one more week and Dad would be officially "unemployed". "On the dole". Despite several tries, he had not found work. Mel passed the Social Security Office on the way to school every day. This was where you "signed on" as unemployed. They gave you some money while you were looking for a job, and also – to some extent – helped you find it. But it was a place that did not give out hope. It looked grim, and smelt of disinfectant and dirt.

Mel was so caught up in her thoughts that she was halfway down the hill before she looked up for Thunderfoot.

All at once, she came to a sudden halt. What was this? A large lorry, of the kind used for transporting animals, was backing through the field gate. Mel's heart almost stopped; was this Thunderfoot's owner at last, come to take him away?

A tall thin woman stood waving her hands about and shouting instructions to the truck driver. Mel broke into a run.

Thunderfoot stood at some distance, head up, watching intently. Mel could see the ripple of muscles on his massive neck. His nostrils flared, sniffing the air. Suddenly, he whinnied and broke into a gallop, thundering up to the woman in a flurry of lumbering hooves. Surprisingly, she did not duck, but stood her ground quite calmly. She began looking him all over.

As Mel came timidly near, the woman stood up. Her face was dark with anger.

"Is this your animal?" she snapped.

"I . . . that is to say . . ." Mel began lamely. The woman took in the bag holding the grooming kit, the halter over one shoulder.

"You ought to be ashamed of yourself," she said furiously. "This horse is in terrible condition. He's half-starved, and his hooves ought to have been trimmed months ago."

Mel stood frozen. Her jaw dropped, but no words came. Suddenly she could take no more. She turned tail and ran off.

At home, Mel flung herself on her bed and burst into tears.

It was so unfair! Mel wept, plunged alternately between misery at one moment and anger at the next. Everything seemed to have gone wrong. That stupid, horrible woman. How could she? How dare she!

Mel was cross with herself, too. What had she been doing, playing at ownership with Thunderfoot? Meanwhile, the horse was suffering, and she, Mel, was to blame. How could she have allowed herself to be so silly? She should have told the RSPCA right at the beginning. She had just wanted to help. "Half-starved," the woman had said. And suppose his feet were really damaged by not having had his hooves cut? Once again her sheer helplessness overwhelmed her. She had been useful to neither her parents nor Thunderfoot. All those good intentions about trying to get a Saturday job . . . completely forgotten. Instead, she had spent a lot of time messing up somebody else's animal. She had foolishly pretended he was her own, and because no one else seemed interested, it almost seemed true.

Although it was only the afternoon, Mel fell into a fitful sleep.

Chapter 7

She was wakened later by Mum, gently shaking her shoulder.

"I left you; I thought you needed some sleep . . . but there's a phone call for you. Do you want to take it now, or shall I tell her you'll phone back?"

"I'll take it," Mel said. "Who is it?"

"I don't know," Mrs Whitby said. "A young woman."

Still sleepy, Mel stumbled downstairs. The voice at the other end of the line was apologetic.

"Hello, my name's Sally Colwynne. Look, I'm terribly sorry about this afternoon. I'm the woman who was so rude to you earlier – about the horse. I realized later that I'd got it all wrong; that you've been coming and grooming and even trying to feed him. I had to find out who you were, and say I was sorry. I asked around, and eventually got you. I'm new round here, you see."

"New?" said Mel.

"Yes, I've just bought Woodforde Farm, by the railway. It needs a lot of work done on it, but I'm hoping to turn it back into a riding stables."

Mel woke up with a jerk. "Oh!"

"Are you still there?" asked the woman on the other end of the line.

"Yes, yes," said Mel, suddenly finding her tongue. "So that's why Thunderfoot was so interested in your lorry; there were horses in it?"

"That's right," answered the woman. "It's

the only field on the farm with a decent fence round it, although there's hardly any grass in it. I've had to put out a lot of feed for them. Your friend Thunderfoot – is that what you called him?"

"Yes," Mel said.

"Good name," said Sally. "Anyway, he's just enjoyed one of my mash specials, and we'll soon have him fat as a school gerbil. As for his hooves . . . Look, I've got a blacksmith coming tomorrow, and I was just wondering, as he knows you, if you'd come and hold him, talk to him."

"Of course," said Mel. "Yes, please!"

"It sounds marvellous," said Mrs Whitby when Mel told her the news. She exchanged glances with her husband. "And don't worry about Dad. We'll manage."

"I'm getting a good bit of redundancy money, so we should be all right for quite a while, even if I don't find a job immediately,"

Mr Whitby told her. "Do you know what that is?"

"Sort of," Mel said. "It's money you get when your job finishes and it's not your fault."

"That's right. It's paying you back for all the time and effort you've put into the job. The longer you've worked, the more you get. I've been working for Mr Fosset for a long time, so I get quite a lot. We'll have to tighten our belts a bit to be on the safe side, but hopefully we won't have to move out of this house or anything."

"Move?" Mel was wide-eyed. "I didn't know you were even thinking of that."

Mrs Whitby hesitated. "We don't think it will come to that, but I'm afraid we still can't rule it out entirely."

"Where would we move to?" Mel asked.

"Somewhere smaller, though you couldn't get much smaller than this house. A flat maybe."

"What about Dot?" asked Mel.

"It would be very hard on Davy, I know,"

Mrs Whitby sighed. "You're older, that's why I'm telling you this. It probably won't happen at all, so let's forget about it. Just be happy about Thunderfoot."

Chapter 8

When Mel walked into the Woodforde farmyard, it was like waking into her daydream of some weeks ago.

Several horses' heads looked out from stable doors. A huge load of hay had been delivered, and filled the air with its sweet scent.

On one side of the yard stood two horses. One was a slender bay mare being attended to by a blacksmith. The other was Thunderfoot.

A voice behind Mel made her turn round. "Hello – Mel Whitby, is it?"

"Yes," Mel said.

"Sally Colwynne." The woman looked quite different now that she was smiling.

Mel shook hands and smiled back a bit shyly; the woman had been very fierce before. She had shortish mousey hair, and wore an old blue boiler suit over jodhpurs and wellington boots.

Thunderfoot turned as they approached and whinnied.

"He's a friendly chap, your Thunderfoot," said Sally. "And he obviously knows you well. If you just stand and talk to him, Mr Thomas here can cut his hooves back for him. We won't shoe him yet or we might frighten him off blacksmiths altogether."

The blacksmith looked up and grinned. "And I don't fancy King Kong here taking a dislike to me."

Sally laughed.

"Oh, I don't think Thunderfoot would hurt anyone," Mr Thomas went on. "You can see he's a real softie. But it's as well to be cautious with a youngster."

Mr Thomas put down the hoof he had just done, gave the horse a friendly slap, and nodded to Mel. Mel took Thunderfoot's halter, and began scratching him behind the ears in the way he liked. The blacksmith picked up a front hoof.

"A youngster?" repeated Mel. "How old is he then?"

"About four, I should think. Just a baby."

As if to prove it, Thunderfoot gave a nervous start and wrenched his hoof away from the blacksmith. Mr Thomas waited a moment before picking the hoof up again and carving off a great slice. Mel talked to the horse quietly. Although he clearly didn't like what was being done to him, he calmed down and let the blacksmith finish the job.

Thunderfoot cheered up considerably, however, when Sally plonked a bucket in front of him.

"Little and often: that's what he needs."

"What is it?" Mel asked, looking at the evil-smelling mush.

"Bran, sugar beet and steamed barley – and a dollop of cod-liver oil." Thunderfoot wolfed it down.

Mel smiled: he reminded her so much of Alice and the chocolate.

"Come into my office. I'd like to talk to you," said Sally. "It's in the kitchen until I can get somewhere else cleared out."

The house looked very different from when Mel had last seen it. A pile of assorted riding helmets tumbled in an ancient armchair. Tall stacks of books stood on the kitchen dresser, amidst piles of papers. Although in a terrible muddle, it looked warm and comfortable.

Sally took a kettle from the side of a Raeburn stove, and put it on the hob. She then stood looking into a box on the floor, placed in the permanent warmth of the stove. Mel followed her, eyes downward. Snuggled up inside the box, and looking like someone who had just won the pools, was the little black cat, and five fat kittens. Two were black all over, two were tabby and one was tortoiseshell, but with a white splash on its nose, just like its mother.

"Spook!" exclaimed Mel.

"Spook?" Sally asked.

Mel explained. "I put food by the gate in the tunnel every time I came. She was so thin when I first saw her." Mel told Sally how she'd come to look for a job with Thunderfoot's owner, and how she'd been terrified by the shining eyes in the empty house – "I thought I'd seen a ghost!" – how she'd found the tunnel gate for once unlocked.

"So it was you who fed her; we wondered how she'd managed on her own," Sally said. "That must have been the day I first saw Woodforde Farm, too. I remember I forgot to lock the gate so I had to go back. I didn't see Thunderfoot; he must have been in the shelter. I still wasn't sure if I wanted the place then, but when I saw it all again, I knew. It was just right."

"I'm glad it's going to be a riding stables again," Mel said.

At that moment, they were interrupted by two fair-haired young men.

"Meet my two brothers," said Sally, "Lexie – and Bruno. They're helping me – mending fences and suchlike at the moment."

"Are you twins?" asked Mel. But this remark caused some hilarity.

"Bruno can't help being stunted: he's like a toad – short and ugly," said Lexie, and ducked a flying wellington.

"How can a toad be nearly six foot tall?" objected Bruno.

"Boys, boys!" attempted Sally. But neither heard. Bruno was listening to the mournful sound of an empty biscuit tin. Lexie cut four slabs of bread and spread them liberally with jam. Then they found the tool they had come in for, and clattered out.

"Those two eat more than all the horses put together," grumbled Sally.

She and Mel each took a kitten onto their laps, and fondled them.

Neither of them spoke for a while. It felt very peaceful. Then Sally got up, and put the kitten back in the box. It mewed lustily, as its grateful mother cleaned it with a firm tongue.

Sally took a scrap of paper from one of the piles, and sat down in front of the telephone.

"And now," she said to Mel, "that I know—" she grinned sheepishly, "—that you aren't Thunderfoot's owner, and you know I'm not, we'd better find out who is."

Chapter 9

She dialled. It was quite a long number; not a local one then, Mel thought.

The woman who answered seemed ill at ease, and reluctant to help.

"I should like to speak to Mr Fearley," Sally said. There was a firm note in her voice. They could hear some kind of argument going on at the other end. Eventually a man came on the line. He too sounded suspicious, and it was with the greatest difficulty that Sally got anything out of him at all. It was obviously inconvenient to be reminded of the horse's existence.

"He left in a great hurry," Sally said later. She found out that Thunderfoot's sire was an elderly Ardennes stallion, who had unexpectedly got into a field with a Shire mare. It semed that although both Thunderfoot's parents were pure, he was held to be of little use because he was a mixture.

"I was going to sell him on but . . . I'm in another line of business now," said Fearley. "He's no good to me. He's not even halter trained. You deal with him. I can't be doing with him now." The man paused, trying after all to make Thunderfoot sound like a good deal. "Put a bit of flesh on him – and you could always sell him for meat."

"Sell him? Meat?" repeated Sally.

Mel turned pale. Of course, that's what happened to horses that weren't much use for anything . . . She should have been warned: the woman in the pet shop had said Fearley mostly dealt in fatstock. And what else could fatstock mean than meat? At that moment, Mel wished she had never set eyes on Thunderfoot. To read about ponies rounded up on Dartmoor and sold for meat is bad enough. To get to know and love a horse which is sold for meat is quite, quite another thing. A great lump rose in Mel's throat. She tried to swallow it, but it wouldn't go away. Thunderfoot . . . meat. She thought of the great head bending to greet her, the soft lips pulling gently at her collar, hoping for tit-bits.

The voice on the other end of the line sounded persuasive. Mel tried not to listen.

But Sally had had enough. "Bit of flesh!" she cried. "There's not enough meat on that horse to feed a cockroach! You left that horse to starve, and starve he nearly did. If it hadn't been for someone giving him the odd bit of food, he might well have died."

Fearley was becoming angry. "Look, I was trying to do you a favour. If you're going to be like that, I'll take him back. I don't care what happens to him, but I'm not going to be pushed about by a snotty woman."

Oh, what has Sally done now? Mel wailed inside. Why did she have to phone Fearley? If she'd just left him, he'd probably have forgotten about Thunderfoot, and everything would have been all right. (Later, Sally told her that this was not so – that men like him never left things alone. Later on – maybe months, or even years later – he would have turned up and demanded the horse back; you could never trust people like Fearley.)

Sally's voice had turned crisp and firm. "You have said that I should 'deal with him', and so I shall. I shall treat those words as a verbal contract, and accept the horse as my property. I shall need to have that in writing, please, I will send you something immediately, and I will expect it back by return of post." She paused, and carried on in a voice that was far quieter, but for some reason, much more powerful. A shiver ran down Mel's spine, a shiver of delicious terror.

"If I don't hear from you within three days,

Mr Fearley, I will report the matter to the RSPCA and the police. These days, maltreatment of animals is treated as a serious matter."

Mel heard the answer, a terrified murmur of agreement.

"Thank you!" Sally almost spat, and slammed the phone down.

Then she flopped into a chair. They were both shaking. "Phew!" said Sally. "That, as you will have gathered, was the man we bought this place from. I haven't met anyone quite as nasty in my life.

"I do hope he does sign the contract I send him," she added with a frown.

"I shouldn't think he'd dare do anything else," Mel said. "That is, I hope he will, too," she added, suddenly worried. "You were pretty terrifying."

Sally laughed. "Yes, I can be quite fierce when I want, can't I. As I'm sure you remember yourself! I was only bluffing when I mentioned the police to Fearley, but I'm pretty sure he doesn't want to meet the police at the moment. Rumour has it that the reason he left here so fast, was that he was found to be selling diseased meat as fit for human consumption. That's what he meant by 'another line of business'. He's probably banned from farming completely."

Mel screwed up her nose in disgust. Diseased meat: how revolting.

Just then, the phone rang. Sally picked it up. "Oh, you again, is it?" she said crossly. "I told you before. I'm not selling." And for the second time she put the phone down sharply.

"Grrr!" she said to Mel. "That man's been on and on at me. He wants to buy the railway field. I told him I can't: that field comes with the track through to my stables, and to all my customers in the town. I can't possibly sell it. I can't think why he didn't buy it from Fearley before."

"Maybe it's a rival crook," said Mel, thinking about Mr Fosset and the dairy. "There seems to be a lot of it about at the moment."

Sally sat for some moments, chin in hands. Then she looked Mel in the eye. She hesitated slightly before saying, "Mel, I would never let Thunderfoot go for meat. But I do have to tell you I can't possibly keep him. He's expensive to feed, and I have no use for a draught horse like him."

Thoughts raced through Mel's head. She wanted to say, you could use him for this, or that, or the other: but she dared not contradict Sally.

Sally understood. "I know it's hard for you," she said kindly. "What we must do is think sensibly about getting him a good home. And the best way to do that is to train him. For a draught horse, that means training him to harness.

"I will also contact a friend of mine who uses draught horses for logging, who might buy him – she lives in Cumbria."

Mel nodded. Sad as it would be, she was beginning to realize that Sally was right.

She pictured Thunderfoot pulling logs about in a leafy wood, sun slanting in between the branches. It sounded good, but Cumbria . . . that was so far away. Wasn't there anywhere nearer?

"Can I come and see him often, before he goes?" Mel asked. Now Thunderfoot would be having a proper owner – someone who would train him properly and look after him – Mel thought she ought not to push in. Sally might not like it.

"Of course you must come," said Sally. "And I've been wondering . . ." She looked at Mel a bit doubtfully. "You said you were looking for a job, didn't you? Getting this place started is going to be an awful lot of work. Would you consider coming to work properly on Saturdays? I can't pay very much, I'm afraid."

Mel choked into her tea. Would she? Help in a stable! And at last, however little, she could offer practical help to Mum and Dad. She'd see Thunderfoot too. Then a problem struck her.

"But I can't really ride!"

"There won't be a great deal of riding at first," Sally answered. "It'll mostly be clearing things out and clearing up. But as soon as I can, I'll teach you."

Chapter 10

The next time Mel turned up at the stables, Sally greeted her warmly. She patted her pocket with a smile. "It's come," she said, and pulled out a stiff envelope.

"The letter from Fearley?" Mel said. "Already?"

"Yes," Sally said. "Thunderfoot's all mine now. All legal and correct."

A wave of relief swept over Mel. Now Thunderfoot belonged to Sally properly, he would always be safe. It wasn't quite the same as owning him herself, but almost as good.

Now there was no chance of Thunderfoot ever going for meat.

Sally was looking at her oddly. "Something's been puzzling me," she said. "Fearley said Thunderfoot hadn't even been halter trained."

Mel blushed.

"Did you halter train him?" Sally asked. "I thought you could hardly ride? Though you groomed him well enough."

"I didn't know he wasn't halter trained either. I just sort of did it. And when anything happened I didn't understand, I looked it up in a book. We were learning together, I suppose." Then with a burst of pride: "And he's awfully clever, you know."

"Anything else?" asked Sally.

"I thought it would be a good idea to train him to my word. He walks and halts when I ask."

"It was a good idea," said Sally. "Well done!"

"And—" Mel hesitated. Now she knew a bit more about horses, she realized it was a very silly thing to have done; it could have been dangerous. "Well – I can't ride properly, but I have sat on his back and walked about a bit."

"You rode him?" Sally said angrily. "A horse you didn't know, who didn't belong to you? You could have been killed. You were lucky. However," she said a bit more kindly, "all that will make it a lot easier to break him. A horse that's been left until he's four years old is often too used to his freedom to be easily trained. But I don't think we'll have any problems with Thunderfoot." She smiled. "I can see you're going to be a very useful asset round here."

After that, Mel visited the stables every day.

Sally wanted to open as a riding school in two weeks' time, so there was a great deal to be done. Mel found herself knocking in posts, scrubbing out water troughs and making endless cups of tea. She learned how to muck out a stable, to mix a bran mash, and how to tack up.

Twice that week, Sally was able to give her a riding lesson.

"For someone who's ridden an unbroken four-year-old giant, you look remarkably nervous," Sally said, laughing.

"But it was different with Thunderfoot," Mel protested. "I knew he wouldn't run off." She felt most peculiar sitting in a saddle; the pony seemed too narrow, and her legs wobbled in the stirrups.

"Don't worry. Pierrot is about as lively as a trussed chicken. I'll be using him for all my beginners."

For all Mel's fears, she was actually doing quite well. All that riding around bareback had given her a good sense of balance.

"Balance is the beginning of everything," Sally told her. "Once you've got that, you can learn to relax your waist and shoulders; then you'll begin to use your hands correctly. You can be quite firm with the legs, but always be gentle with the hands. A horse's mouth is the part you are in contact with; it needs to be kept soft."

Mel nodded: it was something she'd read, but was finding much harder to put into practice.

Thunderfoot was learning, too. Towards the end of the week, Sally decided it was time for him to try a bridle and bit. "Look," she showed Mel. "I had to construct it out of odd pieces; there was nothing big enough in my spare tack box."

Thunderfoot was unhappy about opening his mouth to take the bit. He threw up his head, high out of reach. Mel handed the bridle to Lexie, who was taller. Sally stopped her. "Don't reach up. He might think you're going to hit him." She thought a bit. "Hmm . . . I think we'll have to use cunning." She ran into the house and came back with a jar of honey which she smeared all over the bit. Greed overcame any distrust Thunderfoot might have had, and Mel was able to slip in the bit quite easily.

"We'll leave you to chat to him quietly,"

Sally said when Mel had all the straps done up properly.

Thunderfoot was obviously getting every bit of sweetness out of the honey. Long globules of spit dribbled down his chin. He shifted the bit around, getting used to the unaccustomed feeling. Mel wiped his chin with a handful of straw. Gradually, his ears came forward again, and he began to relax.

A large shadow loomed in the stable doorway. Mel jumped. "Dad!"

Rather against her better judgement, Mel felt embarrassed at seeing him there. She had not told Sally of the problems at home. Sally obviously came from a well-off family; Mel felt sure neither she nor her brothers had ever been unemployed, and that they would not understand. She looked about her, rather hoping no one had seen him.

"I just dropped in on my way home," Mr Whitby said. "I won't be walking back this way from the dairy much longer, so I thought I'd come and see what you get up to here. So that's Thunderfoot. What a splendid beast!"

"The best horse in the stables," said Mel.

"Just imagine," mused Mr Whitby, "how it must have been in the days when horses like that were used all over the country. Man and horse – ploughing fields together, pitting themselves against the cold and rain. I'd like to have lived then."

"Gosh Dad, I didn't know you felt like that about horses." Mel might have started to feel guilty at this point, but she did not. Instead, she frowned. Was he trying to say he wanted a job at the stables? But Mr Whitby hadn't noticed her frown.

"I used to ride quite a bit when I was young," he said. "But it's these heavy horses I really like. And I've always preferred working outdoors, even in a town." He gave Thunderfoot a hearty slap on the neck. "See you later, love," he said to Mel and left.

Bruno helped Mel take off Thunderfoot's

bridle. Had he heard anything? Mel wondered. Maybe it would be better if she simply told everyone.

"Bruno?" she began.

"Yes?"

"Nothing," said Mel. "Nothing important." She couldn't bring herself to tell him – at least, not yet.

She gave Thunderfoot a good feed, and led him out to grass. Through the tunnel, she could hear the sound of a tractor, where Lexie was ploughing the railway field so it could be fertilized and re-seeded. Was there really any place for a heavy horse, these days? Mel wondered. She fervently hoped so.

Chapter 11

On Saturday, Mel burst into the kitchen. "Look!" she waved the money proudly. "My first wages! Here, Mum, Dad, it's for you!" She danced round the table, quite unable to keep still. "Sally said she wished she could give me more; she said I more than earned it." Mel was in an ecstasy of happy pride. Dad took the money gravely, just giving her back her usual pocket money. Mum hugged and thanked her.

Mel remembered: "Oh, Dad, it was your last day. I'm sorry. How did it go?" Suddenly, the amount she had earned seemed pitifully small.

"It was quite a day, really. Rather sad." Mr Fosset had shaken Dad's hand, said he hoped Dad would find work soon, and that he'd enjoyed working with him. Mrs Fosset had cried.

"Good!" said Davy. "I hope she was really miserable."

"Why did he say he'd enjoyed working with you?" Mel said. "He can't have meant it or he wouldn't have stopped."

"Hush, children," said Mum.

"Sssss!" went Alice. She had picked this up from Davy, who had been to a pantomime recently, and found that you always hissed at the baddy.

"Not you too!" Mum said to Alice, and picked her up. "Now you lot, don't be too unkind about the Fossets. I think they were genuinely upset."

But neither Mel nor Davy would believe her. Grown-ups always seemed to stick together.

* * *

The rest of the weekend was wet. Apart from a brief visit to Thunderfoot, the family stayed at home. Away from school and anyone else, it was easier for Mel to forget the "clan" at school, and what Sally and her brothers might think. For a while they needn't remember the outside world. It was good for the family to be alone together for a while.

A lot of Monopoly was played, and when Alice (somewhat to everyone's relief) pulled the board away, they played charades. Alice enjoyed this far more.

Monday came, and with it Dad's first visit to the Social Security Office. Mel and Davy walked with him part of the way. At thc point where they separated, they wished him good luck.

"I hope you don't have to wait too long," said Mel.

"Oh, I'll be all right; I've got something to read," he said, holding up a book.

"That's *my* book! What on earth do you want with *Making and Breaking, a Step-by-Step Approach to Horse Breaking*?" Mel laughed.

Dad looked a bit sheepish. "Oh, I don't know," he said, "I expect I just wanted to know what you're doing with your horse. It all looked quite interesting. And you know I'm quite a fan of his."

Your horse, thought Mel. Oh, if only that were true! It really would be a terrible wrench when Sally eventually sold Thunderfoot.

"The better training you give him, the better home you'll find," Dad said.

Mel smiled at him, thanking him for reading her thoughts. I really must get around to telling Sally about Dad, she decided. Tomorrow maybe. "Goodbye then – and good luck," she said. "I'll be crossing my fingers for you."

That evening, Mel went straight home from school. "Where's Dad? Did they find him a job?"

Mum was in the kitchen, brushing bits of food from Alice's hair.

"I'm afraid not. He was a bit fed up. He had to wait ages this morning, too. There were loads of forms to fill in – he hates that. Then he had to have interviews with various people. He might be eligible for some kind of job training. The trouble is, most of the training is in things he knows he doesn't want to do. Anyway, I suggested he might be of some help up at the stables. He was expecting to meet you up there."

"Oh!" Mel said. "That's a wonderful idea." Then she remembered she still hadn't said anything to Sally about Dad losing his job. Well, she'd know by now, anyway; Mr Whitby was not one to keep quiet about anything. What would Sally think?

Mr Whitby was sawing up a plank when Mel arrived at Woodforde Farm.

"Hello!" he said cheerfully. "I'm replacing

some rotten planks in one of the stables." He looked happier than he had for weeks, and Mel felt guilty at not wanting him there.

"Your horse is out with Sally. She's what's-it-ing him; you know, in a circle."

"Lunging," said Mel, pleased to show off her superior knowledge. But Dad winked, and Mel realized he had been teasing her. "You read the book then?" she asked.

"I did." Dad took the plank he had sawn, and placed it carefully against the wall. He stood and looked at her, arms folded on his chest. "I really enjoyed it. I think I'm beginning to see what you horsey lot are on about. Um . . . Nice woman, that Sally. Tough, but OK."

He meant he'd told her! Well, she could scarcely be nasty, but what did she really think?

Mel smiled a little uncertainly and ran off.

She watched Thunderfoot from a cautious distance: she did not want to distract him.

Sally was not standing in the centre of the circle, as she had been when Mel rode, but walking slightly behind Thunderfoot, on a smaller circle. The weight of the rein was enough to keep him in the circle, without pulling his nose inwards. She guided him from behind with the lunging whip. Thunderfoot was a little surprised to be given commands by someone other than Mel, but Sally's expert hands encouraged him to do the right thing.

"Who-a! Good boy, good boy," she said, stepping in front of the horse to make sure he stopped. She made a fuss of him. "He's doing really well," she said to Mel.

Mel took the bridle from her. She was about to lead Thunderfoot off, when Sally said: "Do tell your father how much I appreciate his kindness. He's being a tremendous help."

Mel looked at the ground at the mention of her father, and didn't answer.

"Why didn't you tell me before?"

Mel was conscious of becoming very red. Sally threw her a sharp look. "You aren't ashamed of him, are you?"

Mel shook her head. She couldn't explain what she felt. Eventually she said in a small voice, "No, not exactly, only I . . . I didn't know what you'd think." Her voice trailed off.

"Come on," Sally said. "What do you take me for? These are hard times for lots of people. And we all know it wasn't his fault."

Feeling a bit better, Mel continued. "I'm not ashamed, but I suppose I am embarrassed. I know I oughtn't to be, but the way all the others at school are – the ones whose parents are all right, I mean . . ." And she told Sally everything. About Mr Fosset and Dad's hopes of being manager, about the "clan", the job in the toy factory, and the absolute helplessness she felt.

Sally listened, nodding from time to time. At length, she said, "I know it's difficult for you at the moment, but perhaps you could think of it like this: I think it's pretty brave of him, coming here. Everyone knows, seeing him, that he's Sam Whitby, who lost his job at the dairy.

That can't be easy. He knows there isn't a job at the moment, so he's spending his time usefully by helping someone else. You wouldn't rather he was out of sight in front of a television all day, would you? That'd be enough to make anyone miserable. He's helping me tremendously here – but he's also helping you."

"Me?" said Mel.

"Yes," said Sally. "I'm a small firm myself, just starting up. I couldn't pay to have all that carpentry done. The most important thing is

this: if my riding school fails, I'll have to sell everything. Including all the horses. And selling Thunderfoot as an unbroken four-year-old . . ."

Sally didn't finish her sentence, but Mel understood what she meant: Thunderfoot would almost certainly go for meat. She felt suddenly very cold. And terribly ashamed of herself. How could she ever have thought Sally wouldn't understand? And what did it matter what people thought, anyway?

Whether Thunderfoot didn't like the tone of

Sally's voice, or whether he was simply impatient for food wasn't clear, but he suddenly dropped his head and booted Sally over with his nose.

Sally laughed. Mel helped her up. She felt an enormous relief, now that Sally knew. Not only did she know, but she had understood. Mel had never stopped believing in her father, but it was good to feel that someone as straight-talking and strong as Sally did too. The others simply didn't matter.

"Thanks," she said softly.

Sally patted her on the back and strode off.

Chapter 12

"We could start working Thunderfoot in long reins today, I think," Sally said to Mel. It was a couple of weeks later. Mel had brought the horse in from the field and was grooming him, scrubbing away furiously at a nasty manure stain on his flank. She stood up in delight, "Gosh, already? That's when we begin to work him from behind, isn't it?"

"I borrowed a driving roller we can use. If you get that on him, I'll show you how it all fits together." Mel took the girth and put it on the horse, making sure she buckled it tightly enough to stay put without making the horse feel uncomfortable. Sally fixed in the reins. They fitted through rings in the roller, and trailed out behind, where Mel picked them up and told him what to do.

Over and over again they made Thunderfoot walk, halt, and walk again, Mel walking behind and Sally at his head to make sure he obeyed. Once or twice he tried to trot off, and once he twisted about so that Mel got in a bit of a tangle with the reins, but on the whole it went well. Sally was pleased with him.

"I've found a cart we can use for training him in later on," and she showed it to Mel – an old farm cart, rather rickety, with two large wheels.

Mel ran a hand over the smooth wood of the shafts. They felt worn and comfortable.

"Maybe your father wouldn't mind checking it over, oiling the wheels and all that?"

"I'm sure he'd love to," Mel said. She was dying to get home and tell her parents about the long reins and the cart. Thunderfoot was really coming on well now – and she herself wasn't doing so badly either. How much she had learned in the past few weeks! That day Mel almost skipped back up the hill to her house.

Mr and Mrs Whitby were in the kitchen, as always drinking tea. Alice sat at their feet, tearing a paper bag into small pieces.

"I didn't see you at the stables, Dad," Mel said. Mum and Dad looked serious.

"What's up?" Mel asked.

"The Social Security Office have found me a job."

"But that's marvellous!" Mel exclaimed. "Aren't you pleased?"

"I need the job," Dad said, "I'm just not sure if I want it."

"But I thought you'd take anything? Don't you have to, or we won't get unemployment money?"

Dad looked suddenly tired, older. "I thought

I'd take anything, too. And you're right about the money. But this job is really awful."

"What is it?" Mel asked.

"I've got an interview in two weeks' time at Keevan's."

"Keevan's? Oh, no!" Mel was shocked. "The chicken processing factory! They kill them there too, don't they? They wouldn't want you to do that, would they?"

"I hope not," Dad said. "I won't know until I get there. The whole place revolts me. But I might have to."

He ran his hands over his face and through his hair, as if pressing his head for ideas. "Maybe something else will turn up."

But they all knew it was unlikely.

"What does Davy say?" Mel asked.

"He's very upset. He's gone upstairs."

"You must never work there," Mel said. "Promise you won't."

Dad stood up. He looked very large in the small room. He began to pace up and down. It was very quiet. Only the sound of Dad's boots broke the silence. One, two, three, turn; one, two, three, turn. No one said anything. Mel could hardly bear it. She watched Dad's face for signs of what he was thinking.

Suddenly, he smashed his fist down on the table with such force that the china mugs jumped in the air. One rolled off and smashed upon the floor.

This was not like Dad! Mel jumped back in shock.

"Oh, no!" Mum knelt down and carefully collected all the pieces. Tears were silently rolling down her face. "Oh, Sam." She spoke so quietly, Mel could scarcely hear.

"I'm sorry," Dad said. Then, "We're going to have to do it, Kathy, aren't we?"

Mum, still kneeling, nodded.

Dad bent down, and picking up a fragment of china, put it into her cupped hands.

He straightened up and addressed Mel.

"We're going to have to move, love."

Mel said, "I knew we might have to. I don't mind squeezing in a bit. It's only really bad for Davy."

But Dad shook his head. He came and took both her hands. "I'm afraid it's not like that. You see, there just isn't work round here. I don't just mean move house. I mean move right away, to another town. London, Birmingham maybe." He carried on, explaining, showing her how necessary a move was, how maybe there'd be another riding school nearby, and that it was just something they couldn't avoid.

As the full meaning of Dad's words sank in, Mel felt as though his fist had smashed not the china, but right into her stomach. "Oh," she said. "Oh."

Mum was putting an arm around her, trying to comfort her with soft words, but Mel could neither feel nor hear anything.

In the soft light of the summer evening, Mel crept back into Thunderfoot's field without saying anything to anyone. She could see six children about her own age on assorted ponies, in the small paddock. Sally stood in the middle giving a lesson.

Thunderfoot came up and nuzzled her in his affectionate, clumsy way. How could she ever bear to leave him? So much had happened in the short time since she'd got to know him and met Sally. She'd learnt such a lot, been so happy. And now all this was going to change. Perhaps they'd be in a city, miles from any green countryside. And the awful thing was that her parents didn't want to leave, but were forced to by events beyond the control of any of them.

It was quite simple really: she was going to have to leave Woodforde Farm, Sally and Thunderfoot. Thunderfoot would be trained and sold, and she wouldn't even be there to see it. She must accept the fact and make no fuss.

Mel twisted her fingers in the horse's long

mane, and buried her face in his warm neck. He smelled sweet and good.

She could hear Sally's clear voice from the paddock. In the stable yard, Spook was taking her kittens for a little totter.

It was going to be hard.

Chapter 13

That evening, the family picked at their supper in silence, each wrapped in his and her own thoughts. Alice whined and Mum snapped at her. Davy sat red-eyed and angry, eating nothing. Dad was ashamed and miserable. How could anything be the same again?

In the cold hours of early morning, Mel tossed and turned in her bed. She had the feeling somebody was shaking her, and that she must no longer be asleep. She lay wondering and dozing. And then it hit her. She'd had an idea.

She sat up in bed and switched on the light. She had to assure herself she was no longer dreaming. She was suddenly wide awake. Was it a good idea? Was it possible? She needed to think. She wrapped a dressing-gown around herself and tiptoed downstairs to the kitchen.

To her surprise, a light was still on. In an armchair, still in his clothes, sat Dad. He was fast asleep but his face was so careworn, so sad.

Mel shook him. "Dad, Dad!"

"Mel?" he said, then realized. "I must have fallen asleep. Is it morning?"

"It's three o'clock," said Mel, "but never mind that. Please listen."

Dad sighed. He wanted to go upstairs to sleep, but he was in no mood to argue.

Mel said, "Maybe I'm mad, but maybe I've got something." She spoke urgently. "Dad, you liked being a milkman, didn't you?"

"Yes, yes of course," Dad said. His mind was still fuddled with sleep. Whatever was the girl getting at?

"And you've got some redundancy money, haven't you?"

"Yes – quite a bit. But we'll need that, I'm afraid, to move. Why?"

"Well," Mel said. "Maybe we won't need to move."

"I'm sorry, love—" Dad began.

"No, no," Mel said, "listen. It's about Thunderfoot, too. You know how hard it is nowadays to find work for a heavy horse?"

"That's right," mused Dad sleepily. "I suppose we're in the same boat."

Mel carried on. "I expect you also know that the thing I'd like most in the world is to keep Thunderfoot. Well, if we buy him—"

"Buy him!" echoed Dad. Was the poor girl going crazy? "What on earth for?"

"Just listen a minute," Mel said impatiently. "I've had an idea that might suit us both. You know how everything traditional is fashionable these days?" She was in a fever of excitement. Her voice rose to a squeak. "Why don't you start your own business with the redundancy money? A milk run. Only don't have any of those nasty electric milk floats that break down and you can't mend. Have a real old-fashioned milk round with a horse. Have Thunderfoot."

Mr Whitby shook himself properly awake.

"By golly," he said slowly. "My own milk business . . . the redundancy money . . . an old-fashioned milk round. It'd be really popular with people! But what about . . ." Then he kept finding problems, reasons why it might not be possible, as grown-ups always do. But Mel was in full flood. Ideas flew from her like streamers from a party popper: she solved every question.

And soon Dad was having his own ideas, and he was full of it too, and any problems Mel thought up, he had answers to.

Over steaming mugs of cocoa, they talked long and hard into the early hours.

When Mum stumbled downstairs to greet a bleak and dreary day, she found instead a blaze of light and warmth.

Delicious smells of sizzling bacon and sausages wafted up through the house.

"One egg or two?" asked Dad, spatula raised, a happy grin on his face.

Mel took a night-sodden Alice from Mum's arms. "I'll change her for you."

"Have you two been up all night?" an astonished Mrs Whitby asked.

Davy appeared. He stood for a moment, idly watching a column of black smoke rise into the air. "Did you try and mend the toaster again, Dad?" he asked with some glee.

Mr Whitby switched round with a loud cry, and turned the toaster off at the plug. He removed a blackened lump. "Bother," he said. "I really thought I'd fixed it that time."

"Never mind," said Davy happily. "Dot quite likes it like that. And bacon rind too! She will be pleased." He found her bowl, and began cutting it all up into peck-sized bits.

Dad made some more toast, under the grill.

Then, over the largest breakfast any of them had ever had, Dad and Mel explained the whole scheme.

"Brilliant!" squealed Davy, bouncing round the kitchen.

Mum was more cautious. "It might work."

Mel crossed her fingers and hoped and hoped they could make it happen. She wouldn't tell Sally yet – not until she was absolutely sure.

She knew – they all knew – that it was still just a good idea. A lot of difficulties lay ahead. They still didn't know if it was even possible.

"What do you think then, Kathy? Do we give it a go?" Dad's voice was very serious now.

Mum didn't answer at first. Even if it was a good idea, she knew it wouldn't be easy. And if they tried and failed, what then? It wouldn't just be a disappointment. They would have wasted all their precious redundancy money. They would have nothing.

She looked round at all the expectant faces. She pictured them penniless, homeless, thrown out on the streets: that is what would happen if they lost everything. And yet – she pictured Dad, a milk bottle in either hand, happy once more.

Perhaps they should at least find out if they could do it.

"We'll look into it," she said. "Yes."

Chapter 14

Right from the start, the problems facing the Whitby family were pretty big ones.

"How are we going to afford this lot?" Mrs Whitby worried. Mel's father looked over her shoulder at the list she had made.

1. Premises – must be near stabling and town.
2. Milk float – could we convert ordinary cart? Hygiene *very important*.
3. Equipment – fridges, crates, bottles, etc.
4. Thunderfoot.

* * *

"Premises would cost the most, of course. Then there's the float. And the fridges – gosh, it will add up to an awful lot."

"There are bound to be other things we'd need," said Mrs Whitby. "The redundancy money would only cover a tiny part of it all."

"Yes," agreed Mr Whitby thoughtfully. "We'd have to borrow most of it from the bank. I've never done this sort of thing before. I don't know what they'll feel about lending to such an unusual project, too. If we can't persuade them to lend us anything, that's it. We must forget the whole thing."

Mum looked troubled. "Banks don't usually like strange ideas."

"We won't lose anything by trying," Dad said. "First they'll want to know how much we need to borrow. I'll find out roughly what it will all come to."

Mel wondered how much Sally would want for Thunderfoot. Untrained he was worth very little – properly schooled and broken, an awful lot. If Sally had already arranged to sell him to her friend in Cumbria, she might feel she ought to keep her promise. It was a horrible thought. Mr and Mrs Whitby had both agreed that they should tell no one about their plans just yet (though Mel had already told Angeline). News in Oxley travelled like wildfire and they wanted to be sure a horse-drawn milk round was really possible before letting everyone know.

There were enormous problems before them. Mel had to admit she hadn't realized quite how large. But at least they had all taken her idea seriously.

Mr Whitby made an appointment with the bank manager after school.

"I have to bring my daughter. She's involved in this too."

The voice on the other end of the line was disapproving – "Mr Grindle is a busy man," – meaning that Mr Grindle would not wish to waste his time with children.

Dad insisted. The voice reluctantly agreed.

"Hmm," Dad said. "I think this might not be easy."

The day before the appointment, Mel was worried.

"If the bank manager thinks it's a good idea he'll give you the money," said Angeline. "I think it's fantasmagorical."

"You're not a bank manager," said Mel. "And if *he* doesn't think it's fantasmagorical, he won't give us the money."

"What are you going to wear?" Angeline asked, to change the subject. But this threw Mel into an even worse panic.

"And Dad! He can't possibly wear that awful jumper. Not to see a bank manager."

Angeline reflected. "My dad's much shorter than yours. But he's a lot fatter. Your father might be able to borrow one of his jackets."

So it was that the next day Mr Whitby and his daughter found themselves ushered into the carpeted silence of Mr Grindle's office. Mel, neat in her best school dress, sank nervously into well-upholstered leather. Dad – showing only a little more shirt cuff than is usual – sat in a chair that squeaked embarrassingly every time he moved.

Mr Grindle was a small, dried-up looking man. He sat and listened to their plans without comment.

I don't think he believes us, Mel thought.

Mr Whitby ground to a nervous halt.

"One moment, please." Mr Grindle went out. Mel and Dad sat in silence, not daring to speak, or even move. They both felt utterly small and helpless.

Mr Grindle returned with another man, who looked even thinner and more sour-faced than he did. "My deputy, Mr Grudge." Mel felt sure neither of them had ever smiled in their lives.

Mr Grudge listened gravely as Dad repeated his story. When he had finished Mr Grudge leaned forward. He spoke slowly and deliberately.

"We hear a great number of requests at this bank – and I know Grindle is with me on this." He paused to blow his nose on a very white, ironed handkerchief. "We think that this is quite simply the most splendid idea we've heard in years."

"We'll certainly be able to offer a good deal of what you'll need," added Mr Grindle.

Have we done it? Am I hearing right? But what did he mean by "a good deal" – what about the rest, thought Mr Whitby.

Mr Grindle continued. "Moreover, I do believe that as you are unemployed, you are eligible for a little financial assistance from the government . . ."

"Do you mean the Enterprise Allowance Scheme?" said Mel, suddenly remembering the sign in the library.

Mr Whitby threw her an astonished glance.

"That's right," said Mr Grindle. He could

see now why the fellow had insisted on bringing his daughter. She certainly had her head screwed on.

"You might have to go on one of their management courses – but that can only be extremely useful to you. They advise you, teach you bookkeeping and that sort of thing. They will give you money every week for a year," and he went on to explain exactly how much. "Of course, it's not a great deal, but everything helps."

It all sounded very complicated, but Dad was nodding furiously, and taking down telephone numbers and addresses.

"We always like to be helpful at the National," Mr Grudge concluded.

Mr Grindle added dreamily, "I remember feeding the milkman's horse when I was a boy . . . I do hope you'll put me on your round."

"And me, and me!" said his colleague.

"You'll be our very first customers!" Dad assured them.

Then Grindle and Grudge bowed their heads in polite farewell, and smiled the sweetest smiles Mel could possibly have imagined.

Mel was walking on air as they left the bank, but Dad looked more serious. "And now", he said to Mel as they took the bus home, "comes the difficult bit: making it all work . . ." He scratched his chin thoughtfully. "Probably the first thing to do is find a building we can use."

Mel was more interested in the purchase of something quite different: Thunderfoot. Now the bank had given them the go-ahead, the thing she had wanted most in the whole world would really come true – at least if everything worked out the way they hoped. The very thought of it made her heart beat faster. Would Sally sell Thunderfoot to them? How much would she want for him? What would she think of the milk round idea?

Chapter 15

It was late by the time they got home and explained everything to Davy and Mrs Whitby. Sally had been out, looking at a horse she was thinking of buying, so Mel would have to wait until tomorrow to speak to her.

First thing the next day Mel raced to Woodforde Farm.

"She's in a hurry," said one old lady to another, as the small figure flew past, dark hair streaming.

"Isn't it poor Sam Whitby's daughter?" said the other. "Shame about all that. I do miss my milk delivery, too."

Mel burst into the kitchen at Woodforde Farm. Sally, Lexie and Bruno looked up in surprise. "Shouldn't you be at school?"

Mel clapped her hand in front of her mouth. "I forgot!" she said. She looked down at their hands curiously. All three held a fat kitten in one hand, lifting up its tail with the other.

"What *are* you doing?" Mel began to giggle.

"We're looking at kittens' bottoms," said Bruno truthfully.

"We're trying to sex them – to see which ones are boys and which are girls," Lexie explained. "So that we can find them homes."

"Come on," said Sally. "Tell us what makes you forget school and arrive here in odd socks on a Thursday morning?"

Mel looked down. It was true. One red sock, one green. She beamed up at Sally, forgetting to explain in her excitement. "I want to buy Thunderfoot. Can I? I mean, how much will he cost?"

Three indignant, still unidentified kittens were thrust back with their anxious mother.

Mel told them her idea. Lexie and Bruno clapped her on the back.

"Thunderfoot – a milk horse! Brilliant!" Lexie said. "He'll read the order book for your Dad. It'll be one neigh for one pint, two for two and—"

Bruno interrupted his brother. "What if everyone wanted six? It'd take forever. And what about yoghurt?"

"Tail for yoghurt, stamping feet for cream. . ." They carried on in this foolish way for some while.

Sally said nothing. She thought for a bit.

Mel held her breath. She hoped Thunderfoot wouldn't be too much. After all, there were so many other things to buy.

Then Sally spoke: "I think I can offer to help. In fact it will solve a number of problems for me too. I've been thinking about this for some time. You've been working for me far harder than I expected, and you'll be even more help as you become more experienced. Your father has helped enormously too.

"If you continue to help on Saturdays, and at other odd times, that should be ample pay for Thunderfoot's feed and shoeing. I've been quite worried recently about selling him, seeing how fond you are of him."

"Us too," said Bruno.

"And to tell you the truth," Sally carried on, "you know the friend in Cumbria who I thought would take him on?"

Mel nodded.

"Well, she told me she can't have him after all. I put off telling you because I was so worried. But this sounds just right for him." She sat down in an armchair, and motioned for Mel to do the same.

"I didn't really buy Thunderfoot; he was given to me as a dead loss. Now I find you need him. I'm giving him to you. He's yours."

Mel was stunned.

"If you smile any harder the top of your head will fall off," said Lexie rudely.

But Mel couldn't even answer him back. She was too happy.

She went to Thunderfoot in his stable and climbed on his bare back. Then she leant forward onto his neck and breathed in deeply. The horse turned round and nuzzled her foot, pulling at it with his hairy lips. Mel was quite convinced he understood. "You're mine now," she told him. "And I'll never sell you. Not even if the milk round never happens. Never, never, never."

"There's that Whitby girl again," said the old ladies. "Going the other way this time."

Every now and then, the small figure gave an extra leap high into the air. The two old ladies exchanged glances. "Must have gone soft in the head," one said, and they moved on up the street, shaking their heads, and making little tutting noises between their teeth.

Chapter 16

This was the start of a very busy time for the Whitby family. Mel worked on Thunderfoot with even more pleasure, now that he was really hers. Mr Whitby got hold of all the people that the bank had recommended, and began a course in business management. At first, he found this so hard that he was almost in despair. Gradually things improved though, and after a few days he started to enjoy himself. In the little spare time they had, they searched for premises. This was far harder than any of them had expected.

There were plenty of places going, but none of them were quite right. Some were impossible; almost falling down and damp. Some were too expensive. Others were simply too far away.

"The trouble is that we need a small office, and lots of decent outbuildings for the fridges and storerooms," Mr Whitby said. "Hygiene regulations are very strict these days – we can't use just any old shed."

"In other words," Mum sighed, "we need Fosset's dairy. It would have been perfect."

"We could at least buy all the old fridges from him. I wonder if they went with the rest of the property? Maybe I'll give him a ring," Dad said.

"Mr Fosset?" said Davy. "Ugh!"

"Ssss!" went Alice. "Ssss!"

Mel opened her mouth to join them in an enjoyable bout of Fosset-bashing, when she saw her father's face and stopped.

"Now, pipe down you lot – he's not so bad as all that," Mr Whitby said crossly.

He's really annoyed, thought Mel, surprised.

Mr Whitby stomped off to phone him.

"Golly!" he said on returning. "This is an unexpected turn of events."

Mel looked at him.

"Mr Fosset hasn't sold after all," he said. "Apparently, that Bullhead chap didn't sign when he said he would, but kept putting it off and off. Then when the milk round had been wound up, and Mr Fosset was getting desperate, he came in and offered much less money. Mr Fosset's in a terrible fix. There was nothing he could about it: what the chap has done is bad but not, apparently, illegal . . ." He smiled. "So I said would it help if we bought the dairy part of the property; he can sell the house quite easily, and—"

"And?" Mum said breathlessly.

"He said yes! Lock, stock and barrel: fridges, everything. He said nothing would give him more pleasure than to beat old Bullhead at his own game. We're in business!"

Dad picked Mel up and whirled her round the room. "By golly, lass, you're a bit heavier than when I last did that! Oh yes," Dad put Mel down. "He says he's got something we must use – he was rather mysterious about it."

An hour later, Mrs Whitby answered the doorbell to Mr Fosset; the children, still unforgiving, had refused.

He stood on the step with a huge box. "Here, you'd better take this," he said, thrusting it into Dad's arms. It was enormously heavy. Mr Fosset had disappeared to fetch another box, equally heavy. "Now, which of these . . . ah, yes," he said, reaching inside one. "This has been hanging around in our attic for years and years. I remember putting it there when motorized floats first came in."

Mr Fosset pulled out a huge circular leather thing, with a ring of tarnished metal round it, and several small rings attached.

"Ah, yes, collar and hames," muttered Mr

Fosset. "Let me see . . . saddle . . . breeching . . . crupper." He began pulling out leather pieces of all shapes and lengths, all wrapped carefully in oiled cloth.

"A harness!" exclaimed Mel joyfully.

Even Davy was beginning to soften, and at Mr Fosset's suggestion began burrowing into the other box.

"Gosh, and there's metres and metres of this stuff!"

"Those are traces – reins," Mr Fosset explained. "There should be a tin of saddle soap in there too." Davy pulled out a flat, round object.

"Look at this picture of a man in a top hat! It must be really old," he said.

"Good quality stuff, that," said Mr Fosset. "It'll soon make this hard old leather as soft as young Alice's bottom."

"But Mr Fosset," said Davy, who was always truthful, "Alice has got nappy rash at the moment. Her bottom looks horrible."

Mr Fosset was thrown for a moment. "Well . . . her cheeks then."

But Alice had heard her name . . . and Mr Fosset's.

"SSSSSS!" she said loudly. "SSSSSSS!" She pointed at him with an accusing finger.

The whole family stiffened in embarrassment. Would Mr Fosset understand? Mr Whitby picked Alice up and took her out. "Talking of nappies . . ." he said. After all, how can you explain to a one-year-old that the bad guy has mysteriously changed into a goody?

But Mr Fosset came from a generation that visited the pantomime every year. He looked thoughtful and the hand with the saddle soap in it froze. "Ah," he said sadly. "Yes, yes, she's right. Children are so truthful. I should have apologized to you all. I – I hoped you'd understand how bad I felt," he looked round at their faces. "You didn't. I suppose I was just thinking of myself, being greedy. Well, I got my comeuppance."

There was a short silence. Then Mrs Whitby spoke.

"It's true you caused us a great deal of upset. But that's all in the past now. In fact it's all working out for the best. Sam would never have started his own business if it hadn't been for you pulling out."

"And I'd never have had a chance of owning Thunderfoot," said Mel, suddenly realizing.

"Thank you," said Mr Fosset, looking relieved. "You're very kind. And of course I'll help in any way I can. First though, I'll show you how to clean this lot up.

And for the rest of that evening, they all sat round chatting, while soaping and scrubbing, polishing and rubbing, until the dark leather was waxy and soft.

The metal was not forgotten either. Soon the dull buckles shone silver and bright. Then they washed it all carefully, and dried it with rags.

Mr Fosset laid it all out carefully on the floor, and showed them where each piece fitted, and what it was for. He told them all the names, and tested Mel and Mr Whitby until they thought they knew it all.

Davy had got bored by this time, and had gone out to see Dot. He came rushing in again, very upset. "There's something wrong with Dot! She pecked me, and she never does that. And she's all scrunched in a corner and won't come out."

"Who's Dot?" asked Mr Fosset. Davy told him. "And she's a Croad Langshan, and she's very rare."

"Do you mind if I have a look at your Dot?" Mr Fosset asked. "I might be able to help. We used to keep chickens."

He followed Davy out to the backyard.

Several minutes later, they came back again, talking deeply. Davy looked a lot happier.

"There's nothing wrong with that hen," Mr Fosset told him. "I'll bring you something tomorrow that should cheer her up."

As he left, he looked round at all of them, as

if weighing up something in his mind. There was a curious expression on his face, as though he was bursting with excitement, but trying to seem perfectly calm.

"Now when does it get dark these days? Right, I'll be round soon after that. And –" Mr Fosset's eyes gleamed, "– I must speak to Emma – my wife, that is – about something. I've another little idea . . ."

Chapter 17

Mel wanted to try Thunderfoot immediately with all the harness. Sally advised her not to.

"Best do everything gradually, one piece at a time. If he becomes frightened by anything at this stage, he may remember it for ever. He's a good-natured horse, and you'll probably be able to go faster than you would with most horses. Don't overdo it, that's all."

Knowing Sally was right, Mel held back her impatience, and did it bit by bit, over several days. The only piece of tack Thunderfoot really objected to was the crupper, which fits under the tail and straps onto the girth, or driving saddle. Tail clamped down, ears back, Thunderfoot cavorted round the stable trying to rid himself of the nasty thing. In the end, Mel fixed a wad of soft sheepskin round the tailpiece, and left him in the stable wearing it for an hour or so. That seemed to do the trick.

Though Thunderfoot was big and strong, Mel realized with fondness that he was just as sensitive as other horses.

That evening when Mr Fosset arrived, Davy raced to meet him. This time, the box he held was small.

"Very careful with this one," said Mr Fosset.

"What's in it?" Davy asked. "Medicine?"

Mr Fosset opened it, and Davy peered in. "Eggs!" he said. "Really brown ones."

"Lovely, aren't they?" Mr Fosset held the box so that Mel could see. There were twelve eggs, ranging in colour from pale copper to an extraordinarily rich conker brown. Others were fiercely spotted and splotched in darkest mahogany.

"They're beautiful!" exclaimed Mel. "What kind of bird laid those?"

"They're from a breed of hen called the Maran, which always lays these lovely eggs." Mr Fosset turned to Davy. "The reason your hen is behaving oddly, is because she's gone 'broody'. This means she has decided it's time to bring up a family. That's why she wouldn't let you take her egg away: she was protecting it."

He stopped, and looked out of the window.

"Hmm, yes, I think it might be dark enough now." He turned to the family. "You don't keep a cockerel, so Dot's own eggs would never hatch. These will." He nodded proudly at the box in his hands. "I've been a long way today to get them."

"Won't she mind them not being hers?" Mel asked.

"No. They'll make her really happy; only we have to be careful. Now, what I'm going to do is quietly slip these eggs under your hen, one by one. It has to be done in the dark, when she can't see anything. Otherwise she'll get frightened and might not sit on them."

Davy and he went off together, Davy holding the eggs as though they were the crown jewels on a satin cushion.

They could hear the occasional squawk and muffled "ow". A few minutes later, Mr Fosset came back shaking his head, a handkerchief wrapped round his hand. Davy was grinning. "Dot still pecked him really hard, even in the dark."

"I hope it means she'll be a good mother," said Mr Fosset, clutching his hand.

"Of course she will," defended Davy. "You could see that. Once she got the eggs, she really liked them. She sort of spread herself out flat, so as to keep them warm."

Dad found Mr Fosset a plaster.

"How long will it be before the eggs hatch?" Mel asked.

"Twenty-one days exactly," said Mr Fosset. "It's not like humans, when you never know when the wretched thing will arrive, causing all sorts of inconvenience. You always know where you are with birds."

"But what are we going to do with twelve more chickens?" pleaded Mum. "We hardly have the space for one."

"Ah – I was coming to that," Mr Fosset answered. "That's all part of my idea . . . may I sit down?

"I'll start with Mr Bullhead's offer on the dairy . . . " He began to tell them how excited he and his wife had been at first: the seaside dream could happen sooner than expected, and so easily! When Bullhead had played such a dirty trick on them, they were devastated. "It meant we wouldn't be able to buy nearly such a nice place as we'd thought," Mr Fosset said.

It also dawned on them how much they

would miss all their friends, and the town they had known for so long if they moved. "But we'd already wound up the business by this time. We couldn't afford to stay, either. It looked as if we were going to have to accept Mr Bullhead's new offer after all. We were trapped. That was when you phoned, Sam." Mr Fosset beamed. "I can't tell you how relieved we were!"

The Fossets' house and garden were still far too big for two. "Of course we could sell it – but then I had another idea," said Mr Fosset. "Now, this is my proposal: it should be quite easy to divide the house and garden in two. If we were to keep the smaller half, how would you feel about renting the rest, with the dairy? Emma and I would much rather have you in there than strangers. I'm afraid it's not all nice and comfortable like this," he gestured round the room. "It needs – and I'm warning you – quite a lot of work. Of course, this will be reflected in the price . . ."

Mum said slowly, "I don't mind a bit of work."

"It would be extremely useful to have the dairy next door," Dad said thoughtfully.

"We'd be nearer Thunderfoot," said Mel.

"Dot would LOVE it!" cried Davy.

"Nice c'oclate!" said Alice, who hadn't understood a word.

"There's one more thing," Mr Fosset said, turning to Davy. "This concerns you, young man. Since meeting your delightful, if – er – fierce, friend Dot, I remembered how much I enjoyed keeping chickens. After all, budgies, chickens – they're all birds, aren't they? Now Davy, suppose you and I breed hens in the orchard, and keep them to sell eggs on the milk round? If –" he coughed in a rather embarrassed way, "– if you don't think I'm interfering in what is now your dairy, Sam and Kathy."

Davy glowed. He looked at his parents with shining eyes. "Oh, Mum, Dad, can I?" Mrs Whitby looked at her husband. He looked at her and they smiled. Then Mum said, "We don't think you are interfering, Mr Fosset. I think it would be a great help, having you next door." More cautiously, she added, "Of course, we'll need to discuss it all first, and we will have to see the place. We'll come and look as soon as it's convenient, Mr Fosset."

Chapter 18

Training a horse properly is a long and painstaking process, for they learn far more slowly than humans. However, this had one big advantage as far as Mel was concerned, as it meant that as time passed, it was she rather than Sally who worked with Thunderfoot most. She felt quite at ease behind him in long reins now. Lately he had been dragging two chains as well, to get him used to pulling something.

"What happens next?" Mel asked Sally. "When do we try him with the cart? Dad's mended it now."

"The cart?" Sally said. "Gosh, we've a long way to go before that. But he's probably ready now to try some more weight behind him. I've got an old tyre that might do. You tack him up, and I'll meet you in the small paddock."

"Why a tyre?" Mel asked, seeing Lexie bring one over. "There are plenty of logs here that would do just as well."

"A tyre drags more steadily," Sally explained. "A log tends to leap about rather, and might

frighten him."

She asked Mel to stand behind Thunderfoot, and take some of the weight of the tyre until he got used to the idea. Two chains ran from the harness, and were attached by a rope to the tyre with a release knot: if Thunderfoot panicked, she could pull this and the tyre would drop off. Lexie took his head. Sally watched.

"Walk on," Mel said, and the horse moved forwards.

Thunderfoot started slightly when he felt

something heavy behind him, but then moved off as though nothing had changed at all.

Soon Mel was able to let him take the whole weight. The tyre slithered after him, bouncing gently over tussocks of grass. Every now and then, the tyre got momentarily caught, and he jerked his head up sharply in fright.

After about ten minutes, they decided he had had enough for a first try and Mel brought him to a halt. Thunderfoot stopped, and turned round to see what had been following him.

"There you are, Thunderfoot, just a boring old tyre, nothing exciting." Mel patted him and turned to Sally. Sally was pleased.

"You're really bringing him on well. I don't think you've got anything to worry about. If he does this several times a day for a while, he'll soon be ready for a cart."

One evening, Angeline turned up at the Whitby household. "I've brought my big brother to see you. You might be able to help one another."

Angeline's half-brother Paul was tall like his sister, and as tidy as she was untidy. He taught industrial design at the local Art College.

"Angeline's told me all about your plans for a milk round. Tell me, do you have a milk float yet?"

"No, we don't," Mr Whitby said. "In fact it's one of the things that has been bothering me."

"Ah, good," Paul Merrell said. "This might work then. I was thinking it would be an excellent project to set some of my students."

"Surely a milk float is a very specialized thing to make?" Mr Whitby said.

"That's why it would be interesting," Paul answered. "For them, it would be a technical exercise. It would give them all sorts of useful problems to solve, and be a tremendous piece to show for their diplomas. People like to see that students can adapt their skills and imagination to the unusual."

Mr Whitby laughed. "Well, it's certainly

that!" Then he frowned. "Won't it be expensive? We were thinking more in the line of an old cart, converted."

Paul shook his head. "To carry glass bottles it'd have to have special wheels and suspension; and nowadays we've got all sorts of exciting new techniques – mainly from designing wheelchairs for disabled people. Then the wooden parts of the float would be done by our furniture design students . . . finished off, perhaps, by a painter. And –" Paul paused for effect, "– and it would only cost you the materials plus a little bit to encourage them."

Mr Whitby turned to Angeline, and grinned. "This was your idea, wasn't it?"

Angeline never blushed. "'Course," she said smugly.

And so it was decided.

Chapter 19

Mrs Fosset was short and plump. "Come in, come in," she said. "It'll be quite something, your taking on the old place. And good luck to you."

What does she mean, "good luck"? thought Mrs Whitby immediately.

They found themselves in the Fossets' kitchen. Davy was very interested in a large cage in one corner, in which a number of budgerigars fluttered and chirruped. Mr Fosset told him all about the different kinds, and showed him the rarest and best.

Mrs Fosset buzzed to and fro, clattering cups and saucers. A smell of warm scones rose into the air.

"More please?" said Alice, sniffing hopefully.

"Silly thing," scolded Mum. "You haven't had any yet."

After a huge tea, Mr Fosset produced a large, old-fashioned key. He handed it to Dad.

"Through that door," he said, pointing, "is the other part of the house. We'll leave you to explore for yourselves, and see if you like it."

They passed through a corridor and into a large, square room. It was rather dark, and an overgrown shrub poked long tendrils through a gap in the french windows. Mel shivered. After the warm kitchen, the place seemed cold, and smelled of damp.

"Look," Mel said, opening a door. "A larder." She shut it again quickly; the smell of damp and fungus was overpowering.

"I've always wanted a house with a larder," said Mum. Mel glanced at her. She too looked disappointed, but was obviously trying to make the best of things.

The next room was worse. They stood in silence, looking up at a large hole in the ceiling, plaster all over the floor. "He wasn't kidding when he said it needed a bit of work," Dad muttered. "What do you think, Kath?"

Mum hauled Alice away from the mess; she was clutching a nail in each pudgy hand. Mum shook her head. "I don't know," she said. Her voice was dull, flat.

Davy was racing upstairs. "Mum and Dad's bedroom!" he shouted down. "Alice's next door! . . . Mine maybe! Oh!" His voice became muffled. "Mel! Mel!" he squealed. Mum and Dad exchanged a sort of "oh dear" look. Mel followed more slowly. It was better, though it still smelled damp. "Where are you?" she called, glancing in at bare floorboards and peeling wallpaper.

"Open the small door at the end."

Mel looked for it. At the far end of the

passage was a door she had at first taken to be a cupboard. She lifted the latch and opened it. In front of her was a little, dark staircase. Then Davy's voice came through more clearly. "Come on up!"

Mel began to climb unpainted stairs that twisted up steeply in the darkness. Suddenly a door opened, and the place was flooded with light. Davy's head popped out. "This is my room," he said excitedly.

Mel entered a small room with crooked floorboards and ceiling sloping almost to the floor.

"See!" Davy said, drawing her to the window. Mel saw a big, overgrown garden, bordered by the railway.

Next to it was the orchard, with a large shed in it.

"Dot's orchard," said Davy proudly. He pulled at Mel's arm. "And this must be your room."

This room was L-shaped with a large old

cupboard at one end, and two rather lopsided windows. These faced at right angles to the other attic room, and directly on to the railway field. Mel saw the old animal shelter, now repaired by Lexie or Bruno. Thin spikes of new grass glowed green against brown earth.

For a moment Mel forgot about the damp downstairs, the fallen plaster, the stench in the larder.

Soon Thunderfoot would be back in the railway field. Mel would be able to lie in bed in the morning and hear the clopping of his hooves as Dad brought him into the yard.

She would bring her desk by the window, and in the evenings she would be able to do her homework, and look out at Thunderfoot, quietly grazing below. She'd know he was both happy and safe.

Mel heard the doorlatch downstairs lifted, and the sound of someone heavy creaking upstairs.

Dad poked his head in. Mel came down to earth again.

"Well, the roof seems OK, anyway," he said, looking round him.

"What a shame about downstairs," Mel said. "Otherwise, it would have been so nice here . . ."

"I've been checking things, and it isn't nearly as bad as it looks. The boiler needs replacing; that's why the ceiling fell, because it leaked everywhere. That probably caused a lot of the damp, too.

"We'd be without heating for at least the first winter, and it'll be a bit like camping at first. It won't be easy with Alice in this state, either. We'll do what we can before we move, but we won't be able to do much at this stage."

"Does that mean we're moving here, then?" Mel said.

"It looks like it," said Dad.

Mr and Mrs Whitby decided that they should move into the dairy as soon as possible. Mum raced off there every morning, returning in paint or glue-spattered clothes just in time to greet the two children from school. Only Alice was causing problems. She strongly objected to being bundled off to a different friend every day: babies are like that.

"Still," as Mum said wearily, "she'll like it in the end."

Dad had almost finished the business management course. It had been extremely helpful, and he felt a bit more confident now about setting up on his own.

In the evenings, Mrs Whitby went to a course on bookkeeping, while Dad cooked supper with one hand and held Alice in the other.

Sometimes Mr Fosset popped round. After drawing up plans for chickens' nesting boxes with Davy, he would advise Dad on which milk supplier to use, and how many milk bottles were likely to break each month. While he did this, Dad would be changing Alice's nappy or checking the potatoes.

It was the start of a very busy, exhausting time.

At least, thought Mel, everything is going well now. Perhaps she should not have been so confident . . .

Chapter 20

It was an ordinary brown envelope, of an insignificant, official type. Mr Whitby thought nothing of it when he opened it. Inside, the letter was on thin paper with a local authority heading. Mr Whitby read it.

"It has recently been brought to our notice, that an attempt is being made to re-open the dairy at 1 Woodforde Farm Lane.

"A complaint has been made regarding the altered nature of such an establishment. If we are correct in our information that a horse is to be used on, or near the said premises, we have to inform you that permission must be sought and granted before this could be allowed. (Reg. 25117, *Department of Health Booklet 716*.)

"We must also remind you that the sale and despatch of foodstuffs are subject to clear regulations.

"A Department of Health Inspector will be sent upon receipt of application, and a report will be made."

"What does it mean?" Mel asked fearfully.

"It means that we may be in trouble," her father said. "They seem to think that if we are using a horse, we may be breaking some law or other; I suppose laws could have changed since horses were used on milk rounds before."

"'Permission must be sought and granted'," quoted Mrs Whitby. "I don't like the sound of that. What do we have to do to get permission? Who decides it? And what are the regulations?"

Mr Whitby scratched his head worriedly. "I wish I knew," he said.

"Whoever could have made a complaint?"

Mel wondered. "It's really creepy, having someone go behind your back like that."

"I don't know," Mr Whitby said. "I wish I did, then we might know what we were up against."

"Maybe it's just routine," Mum said.

"No," Dad said. "Look at the letter: 'a complaint has been made'. Somewhere, somehow, we have made an enemy."

"I'm worried," Mum said. "It all sounds so – so official and important. What can the inspector do? Will he just tell us what's wrong so we can put it right? Or is using a horse completely out of the question nowadays?"

"But they can't stop us from opening," Mel said. "Can they?" She looked at her parents. Neither of them would speak. They exchanged glances.

"Tell me," Mel pleaded. Everything had been going so well up until now. Was it possible it should all fall through because of some stupid regulation?

Mrs Whitby spoke carefully. "I think we should all stay calm – it may not be important at all."

May? thought Mel. That means it may be important.

She'd promised Thunderfoot she would never sell him, whatever happened. Now she realized how fragile that promise had been. One little letter, and everything could end: the milk round, Dad's job, Thunderfoot, everything. She felt suddenly very weak. Her legs had turned to jelly, and she sat down on the nearest chair.

Davy was crying.

"Your mother said to stay calm." Mr Whitby looked round at them all. "It won't do any good for us to panic. This afternoon I won't come with you to the stables, Mel. I need to understand more about this. I'll go down to the Town Hall and see what I can find out."

At school that day, Mel couldn't concentrate at all. In the evening, when Dad returned home, even he was gloomy. Permission to open, it appeared, had to be granted by the local council. And although Dad had put in a request immediately, it could not be discussed by them until several meetings ahead – just a week before they were due to open.

Chapter 21

Department of Health Booklet 716 confused them all. It was written in such a complicated way that even Mr Fosset, who was used to such things, found it difficult to understand. But it did look as if they might be breaking a hygiene law. This was made worse by the fact that it looked as if they had been trying to sneak in without proper permission.

"Couldn't you put off opening for a few weeks?" suggested Mr Fosset.

Mr Whitby shook his head. "If we delay anything, we will run out of funds – we just have to get some money coming back into the business as soon as we are able."

Mr Fosset raised his eyebrows. "You do know who the chairman of the council is, don't you? The people who have to give you permission?"

"No," Mr Whitby said.

"Well, I don't want to worry you, but I'm pretty sure it's that Bullhead fellow."

"What, the one who tried to cheat you out of the dairy?"

"The very one."

"But he shouldn't be chairman of the council – not if he cheats," Mel said.

"Maybe he shouldn't, but he is. And don't forget he didn't *exactly* do anything illegal. He's a powerful man, Bullhead. I don't think he liked it very much when I changed my mind about his offer. He's the sort of man who is used to getting his own way, and will go to any lengths to do so . . ."

"So it was him who sent the letter!" Mel said.

"Maybe, maybe not . . . he's got friends in all sorts of high places, that man."

Dad frowned. "It's very fishy, you know. I'm sure there's more here than meets the eye. Well, I've done all I can for the moment. We'll just have to keep getting ready as if nothing had happened. But I must say I don't like it."

The Whitby family had already had a very hard few months. It was not easy to just put a brave face on things and hope for the best. But what else could they do?

"Who-ah boy!" Thunderfoot tossed his head and snorted. Mel watched hopelessly as the horse bucked and plunged, disobeying her orders completely. She was lunging him in full harness with the tyre flying out behind, making him even jumpier. She was terrified lest he should snap something. Although Mel was learning fast, sometimes her lack of experience told against her. And with this new threat hanging over them today she was finding it hard

to concentrate. Thunderfoot felt this; it was sheer mischief.

"Whoah!" Mel said again, knowing it was useless.

Sally came over. "Don't try and stop him, now: he's not listening. Just let him carry on until he's bored. When he slows down to a walk, then say 'wa-alk'. Pretend that's what you wanted all along."

"But it isn't what I want!" Mel protested. "He's so strong, I can't hold him."

"That's why you have to use cunning," Sally said. "You will never match him in strength. But don't give any commands you know he won't obey, otherwise he'll think they don't mean anything."

She stood watching, while Mel tried again.

"That's right, just keep him going . . . a bit longer . . . he's beginning to get tired now . . . keep on . . . I think he's probably had enough now."

Puffing and blowing, the horse eventually had to admit defeat. Mel gave him the command, and gladly Thunderfoot came to a halt. Sally petted and praised him.

"It was partly my fault," Mel said, and she told Sally all about the letter that had arrived, and that it might mean the end of all their plans.

Sally looked very serious. "Are you sure it was this Marshall Bullhead chap who wanted to buy the dairy – the man who owns Freshco?"

Mel nodded. "And we think he's the chairman of the local council who have to give us permission."

Sally's eyes widened. "He was also", she said quietly, "the man who wanted to buy the railway field from me. Don't you remember? He phoned up once when you were there."

"I remember," Mel said. "Perhaps he wanted to live in the dairy, and have a bit of land to go with it – for a horse, maybe." It seemed a likely idea.

But Sally frowned and shook her head. "I don't think so, somehow. He's not a horsey sort of man. I'd know him if he was. Your father was right – it's all very odd." She thought for a bit. "And you say the inspector won't be coming until just before you open?"

Mel nodded. "Mr Fosset said these legal things always take ages."

"Hmm. And I'll bet this Bullhead chap knows delaying things would cause you problems. Well, two can play at that game."

"What do you mean?"

"My father knows someone on the council, too. I'll explain your problem to him – see if he can't get them to hurry it all up a bit. That would help, wouldn't it? He won't be able to change things if you are breaking a law, but at least you won't fail because you run out of money."

All this time, Thunderfoot had had his head down and was munching away at the grass. Sally gave him a hearty slap. "As for you, my lad, I think we might cut out the mash specials from now on. Just bulk – hay and grass now." She turned to Mel. "I'll let you know as soon as possible about the other thing."

Dot's eggs hatched the day before the Whitbys were due to move into the dairy. Davy paced up and down in front of her coop like an expectant father. But Dot wouldn't let him near. She spread herself out quite flat, and glared at him angrily, ready to peck if he got too close. Davy thought he heard a high-pitched peep-peeping,

but wasn't sure. He couldn't hear because Dot was making a funny "brrring" sound. He suddenly realized that this was the first noise he'd heard from her in twenty-one days.

Mr Fosset came round that evening.

"I thought I'd better bring a glove this time." He reached under the furious Dot, and brought out a tiny, still wet chick. It was still so feeble, it couldn't stand. Davy held it in eager, trembling hands. Mr Fosset made him put it back, and fished out another. This one had hatched earlier, and was all fluffed out. It peeped loudly and struggled, and it was all Davy could do to hold it. It wasn't yellow all over as he had expected, but black and grey too, with a fluffy yellow behind. Davy thought it was the most wonderful thing he had ever seen.

By the following day, when Mr Fosset arrived to help take Dot to her new home, Davy was sure that all twelve eggs had hatched.

"That's excellent," Mr Fosset told him. "Not a single dud."

"I told you she was going to be a good mother," Davy said smugly.

Mel looked round at the house she had lived in for as long as she could remember. Already it looked cold and unfamiliar. Were they doing the right thing? It was awfully scary, the way they just had to keep going. What would happen if the council refused them permission? It suddenly hit her: an overwhelming feeling, like jumping onto an already moving roundabout. They could not stop the machinery now, even if it was going to lead to disaster.

Mel swallowed hard and set her teeth. Round her, the rooms stood bare, with all the family's belongings packed into chests. All the carpets were rolled up, the furniture stacked out of the way.

In a moment Lexie and Bruno would arrive with a furniture van. Mum was over at the new house already, having a final clean-up. Davy and Alice were with her.

Dad came in, his boots echoing in the empty room.

"Bit sad, isn't it?" She could see the worry in his eyes, though he spoke lightly.

"A bit," she agreed.

"Look what I found. It must have dropped down behind something."

Mel shook her head, unable to decipher the childish scrawl. "What is it?" she said.

"It's a horse, of course. The first one you ever drew. See – there's the head . . . legs . . . tail."

"Oh yes. I don't remember. Did I like horses even then?"

Dad put his arm round her and smiled. "Always. It took me years to find out just how much: with your help." They looked at one another, sharing their fears for the future. It was good to share them for once. Their lives would all be changed: for better or worse?

Outside there was the sound of a lorry drawing up.

"They're here!" Mel said. They were off.

Chapter 22

The Whitby family settled in quickly. There was so much to do, that they had little time to stop and worry.

Mr Fosset and Davy had cleared out the shed in the orchard, and fixed perches and nesting boxes inside. Davy had lined the boxes carefully with straw, and put a white china egg in each, to encourage new hens to lay there.

"Dot's chicks won't be laying for ages yet," he told his mother. "So we've ordered fifty point-of-lay Warrens; they're the ordinary kind of brown hen they use in batteries. They don't look much but they lay like anything, Mr Fosset says."

Mrs Whitby smiled. "And 'point-of-lay'? What does that mean?"

"It means", said Davy importantly, "that they are the right age to begin laying eggs – Mr Fosset says." He skipped off to see Dot and her chicks again.

Dot could scarcely believe her luck in being given free run of the orchard.

Davy saw how she found food for the chicks, making a special noise so that they came running up expectantly. She caught insects, stunning small ones with a sharp peck, chopping up large ones and handing them out fairly. That way, the chicks learned how to catch live food. Mrs Whitby couldn't bear to look, but Davy lay on his stomach in the long grass, and watched them for hours.

Moving in takes time when you are doing it all yourselves. They were still surrounded by tea chests and mess when the second letter arrived. Mrs Whitby opened it.

"Goodness," she said. "The inspector is coming tomorrow!"

Dad puffed his cheeks out and then blew out the air with an expression of horror. "Just look at it!" he exclaimed, surveying the chaos surrounding them.

"And the council will decide the day after," continued Mum, jumping up. "Come on, we've no time to waste! Forget the house for now – we don't mind sleeping-bags again – grab the buckets and scrubbing brushes everyone! To the dairy!"

"Sleeping-bags again?" said Davy. "Goody!"

The family set to. Sally sent Bruno and Lexie over for a bit, and even Angeline turned up to help (though, as she rightly put it, "housework isn't my strong point").

Every bit of dropped plaster and paint had to be scraped away before they could even begin on cleaning. The fridges had to be scrubbed and disinfected, the outhouses prepared for storing milk-crates and boxes of orange juice.

In the room that was to be Mum's office, they dragged in an old table and cleaned and polished it with nice-smelling wax polish. At the windows, they put up some rather pretty blue and white curtains Mum had picked up at the Oxfam shop. Most important was a second-hand but still smart computer.

"You can have your old-fashioned milk round, but I'm going to be absolutely up to date with my bookkeeping," Mum said firmly.

By three o'clock the next day, the whole dairy had been transformed. It gleamed, it sparkled, it positively shone with a luminous glow of cleanliness.

The inspector was a thin-lipped woman with hard permed hair and too much make-up. Alice immediately started hissing at her, and had to be whisked away. Mel and Mr Whitby watched with their hearts in their mouths as the woman went carefully through the dairy, searching every corner, opening every cupboard and door. She missed nothing.

Finally she asked, "The horse will be coming to the yard here, will it?"

Mel gulped: this was going to be it.

"Yes," Mr Whitby said. "I'll load up first, then back him in. We'll be keeping the float in there next to the fridge store." He pointed.

The woman nodded and frowned. "I see," she said. "And will you be bottling on the premises?"

"No," said Mr Whitby. "A lorry delivers the milk much earlier, already bottled."

"Well," said the woman, "I'm rather concerned that there isn't a padlock on the fridge store. The fridges are quite big enough to walk into and it could be very dangerous – I believe I saw a small child earlier?"

"Er – yes, Alice," Dad said. "Yes, of course we'll get a proper childproof lock on that."

"As for the hygiene regulations," the woman

said, "as you are not bottling on the premises, I don't see any problem."

"And what about the council meeting?" asked Dad.

"I shall tell them it is one of the cleanest places I have seen – they can't possibly object to that."

"You mean we can open?" Mel said. She could hardly believe her ears. Was it going to be all right after all?

The woman smiled. "As soon as you like," she said.

In the doorway, about to leave, she turned to them and said, "I shouldn't really tell you this but . . ." she hesitated, "I had a telephone call this morning. I was told that if I did not give you permission I would . . . receive a large sum of money. Of course I took no notice, but . . ."

"Thank you for telling us," said Dad.

"Just be careful, that's all," said the woman.

After that, Mel spent every moment she could at the stables.

"You must make sure that Thunderfoot is absolutely used to traffic," Sally insisted. "We can't have him getting alarmed and causing accidents." So every day, Mel led him out around the town.

The horse had calmed down considerably since cutting out the richer food, and Mel felt quite happy with him on the roads now. She must have walked miles, up and down the steep town streets, and now she knew them almost as well as her father did.

Sometimes Mr Whitby took Thunderfoot out. He had become very fond of the horse over the past weeks. "I'm looking forward to this job so much," he told Mel. "It won't be long now: everything is going ahead so fast."

In a large shed at the stables, Paul Merrell and four students worked on the milk float. No one else was allowed in. They seemed to be there at all times of the day and night. "Nearly ready?" she asked Mr Merrell. "Oh no, not yet," he told her.

Mel became anxious. Not only did the milk float have to be ready, but Thunderfoot too. Would it all be done in time? They hadn't even tried him in front of a cart yet.

Sally laughed at her worried face. "We'll do it," she said, "but you're right. We ought to get a move on. You've just taken him out, haven't you?" Mel nodded. "It might be a good time to try now – he won't be too bouncy after some exercise. Now, which of my brothers is strongest, Mel?" Sally asked her.

"Me!" said Lexie and Bruno at once.

"Right," said Sally. "Then you can both help Mel by dragging that cart out for Thunderfoot."

Mel knew this was the most important part of Thunderfoot's training: it was the moment they had all been waiting for. If things went wrong at this stage, and he became scared, he would always associate a cart with fear. Horses are simple creatures, but they do not forget. They hate feeling trapped, and this is just what being strapped into the shafts must feel like. Worse, there is the noise of the wheels right behind them that they cannot get away from.

This time there was no rope with a release knot: no way out if Thunderfoot panicked.

Mel backed Thunderfoot in towards the cart, while Bruno held the shafts up out of the way. They had to persuade him into just the right position so that the shafts wouldn't hit him when they came down into place.

Talking to him quietly, they buckled all the complicated straps into place. This time, Bruno took his head, while Sally stood in the cart, holding the reins. For this very important moment, Mel allowed the more experienced Sally to take over. Mel and Lexie watched.

The cart creaked horribly. The wheels bounced and rattled over the yard.

Mel's heart was in her mouth as Thunderfoot took his first faltering steps. His head was up, and his back humped. His ears were flat back. Sally spoke to him encouragingly.

At the corner of the barn where they had to turn, he didn't seem to know where to put his feet.

"Poor chap," Lexie said. "He's all over the place. He's got to learn how to manipulate the cart properly, and it isn't easy."

Sweat broke out on Thunderfoot's neck, but he was trying hard. Up and down they went. Bit by bit he seemed less nervous. His back lost its stiffness, and his head went down. Soon the ears came forward, only flickering back when Sally spoke to him.

"Look!" said Lexie excitedly. "He's really putting his weight into the collar now."

Thunderfoot was beginning to enjoy himself. "At last," he seemed to say. "At last I'm doing what I've been bred for."

At last, thought Mel, and it seemed as if a great weight had been lifted from her mind.

"Do you want to try now?" called Sally, and Mel climbed up beside her, and took the reins. It was a great moment.

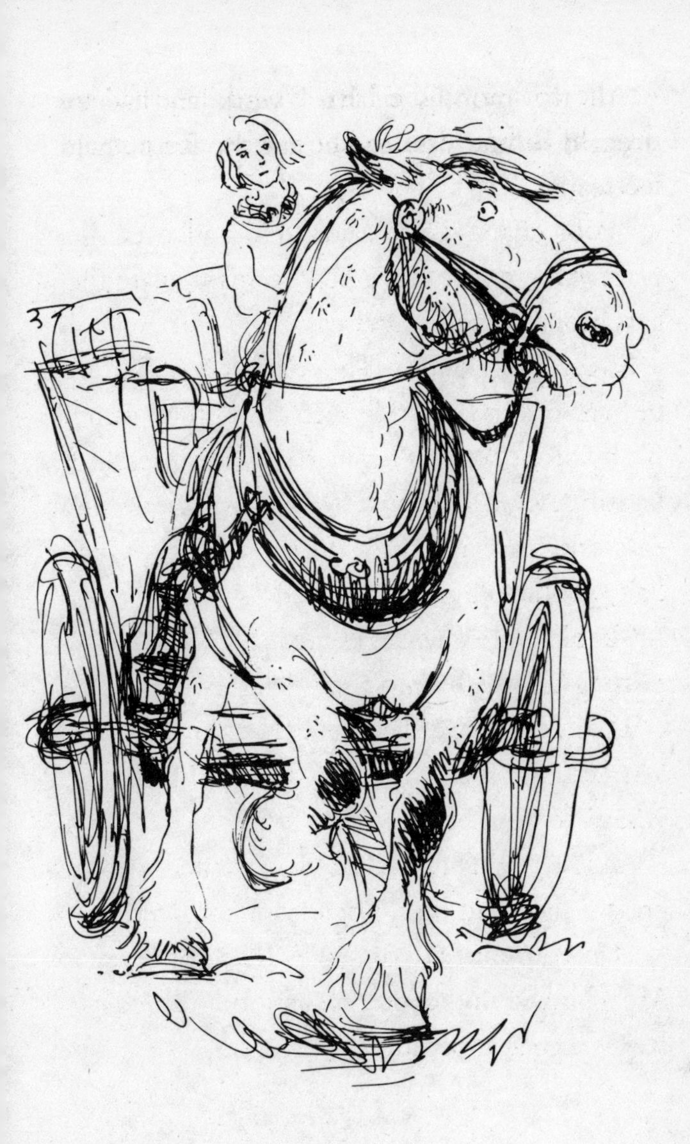

All the months of hard work and worry seemed behind her, and at last the future held no fears.

Chapter 23

"Do you have any old milk crates I could borrow?" Mel asked Mr Fosset one day. "I need to put them on the old cart, with bottles in, to get Thunderfoot used to the rattling."

Mr Fosset took her to a shed and showed her where she could find both crates and bottles. He helped her put six or so onto the cart, and fill them up with empty milk bottles. Thunderfoot stood with head drooped, waiting sleepily.

On the side of the cart was a big sign, painted

by Mrs Whitby. In large red letters, it announced: Whitby and Family's Real Old-Fashioned Dairy. Opening Soon. Place Your Orders NOW!" Word had got around Oxley and they had already had a few orders.

"How is the milk float coming along?" Mr Fosset asked. "It's the Big Day quite soon."

"Two weeks to go," Mel said.

The time seemed to be flying past. Angeline's half-brother and his students had been working on the float day and night, in one of Sally's outbuildings. Dad had been helping too.

"They say they'll be ready in time," Mel carried on, "but only just. They're being very secretive about it: won't let me in to see."

"Hmm," Mr Fosset said. "It's a pity you have to use that old cart. It will be much noisier than the new float would be, and Thunderfoot might be a little alarmed."

Mel smiled at Thunderfoot fondly. "Look at him," she said. "Does he look as if anything would bother him?"

"No," Mr Fosset had to admit. "He doesn't."

Mel took up the traces, hopped onto the cart and drove off.

To her surprise, Thunderfoot woke up immediately. He had just been shod, and his hooves felt tight and strange. Then there was that nasty rattling noise behind him. He wanted to turn round and see what it was, but Mel wouldn't let him. Mum had taken Alice to a mother and toddler group near where they used to live. Mel wanted to go over there and show Mum how good her sign looked.

Thunderfoot put his ears flat back, and kept them there, but Mel didn't notice. After a little while she felt confident enough to go a little faster. Thunderfoot broke into a spanking trot.

All went well till they turned a corner, and into the wind. Horses are often excited by the wind. This was worse. The wind whistled over the empty milk bottles making each one sound a loud fluting noise. Whooooooooh! It sounded like a ghostly choir of wailing spirits. Hooooooooh! Hooo hooo hooooo!

Mel nearly jumped out of her skin and poor Thunderfoot had the shock of his life. He took off at a wild gallop.

"Stop!" Mel screamed. "I mean, whooah!" She clung to the cart desperately as it plunged and rattled up the road and down through the town. It was all she could do to stay on, and it was only sheer luck that enabled her to keep hold of the reins.

"Oh, please stop!" Mel cried.

But Thunderfoot had got the bit between his teeth, and wouldn't listen to her feeble tugging now. The cart rattled and banged on the uneven surface.

If only she could get Thunderfoot to turn away from the town centre, she might have some chance of stopping him on a quieter road. But the horse seemed determined to do his worst. Sparks flew up from the tarmac, as his gigantic hooves pounded along.

Once over the hill, they drew out of the wind, and the bottles ceased their ghastly wailing. Mel tried again to stop him but Thunderfoot tossed his head and carried on. She had a suspicion that he was no longer frightened, but rather enjoying himself.

They galloped straight up the main road, and into the High Street. At the corner, a crate flew off. Smashed bottles rolled all over the road.

Everywhere, people turned and stared, open-mouthed. Cars screeched to a halt and hooted. Mel wished Mum's beautiful sign was not in such large, red letters. Thunderfoot slowed down to a trot. Finally, by a smart yellow lorry delivering vegetables, he came to a halt. He stretched his neck out, and began eating lettuces. Mel felt quite unable to stop him.

The beautiful sign was torn and muddy. Shakily, Mel got off the cart. Quite a crowd had gathered. They laughed to see Thunderfoot polish off the lettuces, and start on the courgettes. Best of all, Thunderfoot decided,

ALMERS

were the exotic fuit. Pawpaw, mangoes and kiwi fruit: delicious!

"Smile!" said a voice, and Mel turned, to find herself the subject of a photograph. It was the last thing she wanted. Mel wanted to curl up and disappear into the ground.

But her troubles were not finished yet. Several people in yellow overalls ran up. "Get that horse away from that fruit! It's the property of the Freshco Supermarket!"

A bulky man in a pin-striped suit pushed his way through the crowd. His face was red and angry. He noticed the remnants of Mrs Whitby's sign, and a flicker of triumph ran over his face. Mel saw it and was afraid.

"Get some men in to remove that fruit," he ordered thc others. "All of it. There might be germs on it. Don't mind the expense; it's our customers I'm thinking of."

"So, it's our little milkmaid! You've had it now. I'll be able to finish you with this," he muttered to her, grinning nastily. Then turning, he addressed the assembled crowd. "It is a ridiculous idea having a horse delivering milk nowadays. They are unhygienic, and – as we have all just seen – dangerous."

"I'm sorry," Mel mumbled. "I'm really sorry; it's all my fault." She took Thunderfoot by the bridle and shakily led him home.

She could feel the eyes of the crowd, and of Mr Marshall Bullhead, burning into her back.

Chapter 24

Who would have confidence in the Whitby and Family Dairy now? Thunderfoot's wild career through the town had been seen by hundreds of people.

Suddenly, Mr Whitby's confidence evaporated. It would be a piece of cake for Mr Bullhcad to "finish them off" now, as he had sworn to do. Everyone said he was a powerful man who always got his own way – and they knew he would use any method, honest or dishonest. He would bring up the subject at the next council meeting. Even if they had passed the hygiene regulations, it would be easy to persuade the other councillors against them now on safety grounds. Sally couldn't save them this time. Apart from that, it was terribly bad publicity.

The whole family felt leaden with disappointment and worry. Mum and Dad tried to hide their misery from Mel, but this made it even worse for her. It was her fault and she knew it. Even Angeline's cheerfulness sounded forced. "Maybe it won't matter," she said.

That afternoon, the man delivering chicken food said to Mel, "Oh, it's you, is it? I saw your picture in the paper! Something about a horse gone wild, wasn't it?"

Mel turned white. Until now, she had completely forgotten the photograph taken of her.

"What did it say?" she asked fearfully.

"Something about a dangerous horse destroying a whole lorry-load of fruit. How on earth did he do that?" asked the man, without waiting for answer. "It said the man from

Freshco was going to sue you for all you're worth. Is that right?"

"Yes," said Mel miserably, "I expect it is."

"In that case," said the man, "can you pay me for the chicken feed right away?"

Stony-faced with fury, Dad paid, and the man went away. Already, it seemed, they were suffering the consequences of Thunderfoot's unfortunate bolt.

If only I had listened to Mr Fosset, Mel thought over and over again. If only I hadn't been so over-confident; none of this would have happened.

Just then, the phone rang. It was for Mel.

"TV News West-Wide here. I'd like to do a piece on you for this evening's news programme. Are you going to be in tonight?"

"Yes, but I don't want—" Mel began.

"Lovely, lovely, that's great then. See you later. 'Byee!"

Mel found herself holding a dead phone.

Chapter 25

"I'm not coming down." Mel put her head under her pillow. She didn't want to talk to anyone, let alone be interviewed and made to look stupid in public. She'd caused enough trouble already; whatever she said was bound to make it worse. The whole thing terrified her. There was a thundering on the stairs. Despite herself, Mel looked up. It couldn't be Mum or Dad or Davy: none of them made that much noise.

"Angeline! What are you doing here?"

"Come on, they're here," Angeline said,

grabbing her arm and pulling her downstairs.

"I can't. I've nothing to say!" Mel protested.

"Yes, you have. I told them to come. I told them what happened, what a swine the supermarket owner was. I said they should phone Sally if they wanted the truth about Thunderfoot, and they did and here they are!"

Mel wouldn't believe her. She shook her head. "No."

Angeline stopped dragging Mel, and turned round. "Look, Mel," she said. "Don't you see? You've got to. OK, so you did muck things up. Now you've got to un-muck them. It's not only you who stands to lose everything. It's your family, Thunderfoot, and Sally too; bad publicity for one of the horses from her stable won't do her any good either. This is your chance to put things right."

"I'm bound to make things worse," Mel said.

"No you won't. You've made them as bad as they can be," said Angeline with typical bluntness.

"Just tell the truth. You'll be fine." Angeline could see her friend was about to give in. "Come on."

"But I haven't even brushed my hair!" wailed Mel. "I must look awful."

"Tripe!" said Angeline. "Compared to me you look like a Barbie doll; they'll sort you out anyway. Hurry up. I told them to go over to the stables. Sally's getting Thunderfoot ready."

Mel had no time to worry further. In Sally's kitchen, two girls were already dabbing Dad with make-up. Davy sat looking clean and scrubbed, wearing a foolish grin. Even Alice had a ribbon in her hair.

"Just a dab here," said the girl. Mel sneezed. The make-up brush tickled horribly. In the yard, Thunderfoot stood surrounded by people, lights, cameras and yards of different coloured cable.

"Stella Hanwoods – I'm the producer," said a pleasant-faced woman, stepping forward. "We just need to do a few tests first. Here's Tony.

He'll be interviewing you." Lights flashed on and off. Cables wreathed themselves about like live spaghetti. Microphones squealed

"Gosh," said Mel. "I've seen you on television!"

The man called Tony smiled. He chatted comfortably to Mel, and she began to feel quite at home.

"Now," said Stella. "Would you all stand here, next to the horse. Sound! OK. Lights! OK. Tony? Right, camera! Take it away."

The camera rolled.

"And now," said Tony, "we come to a most unusual item . . ." At that moment, Thunderfoot put out his head and sniffed Alice, who was being held in Mum's arms. Alice burst into shrieks of laughter, as Thunderfoot's hairy chin tickled a plump stomach exposed by wriggling. "You may have heard", Tony was having to raise his voice over the noise, "about the horse that ran wild through Oxley yesterday."

"More! More!" squealed Alice.

Thunderfoot was certainly playing to the camera.

"Aaaah!" cooed the two make-up girls in unison. "Isn't he sweet!"

Sally spoke a little bit. She said that although many horses would be ruined for a long time by an experience like Thunderfoot's, she thought that he would not: he was normally an exceptionally calm, sensible horse. In the background, Alice was fighting to get Thunderfoot under control.

"Does this horse look dangerous?" said Tony. "Does he look wild?" He got Mel to explain how she had found him half-starved and neglected, how she, with Sally's help, had broken him. He told how the previous owner had said that the only use for him was meat, but how Mel had thought up the idea of a milk round. Alice, feeling ignored, was roaring with anger now.

"A real old-fashioned round, using a horse," shouted Tony. "This solved in one the problem of both her father's unemployment – and the horse's!"

Unfortunately, his little joke went unnoticed, as everyone was watching Alice. With all the crying, her nose had started to run. Mum looked about her desperately for a tissue.

Mel blushed and looked awkward, but Angeline, who had somehow got in front of the camera too, interrupted. "And it's going to be brilliant, and you've all got to put in lots and lots of orders for the Whitby and Family Dairy, Telephone 45361."

"Er, OK, OK," muttered Tony. They weren't supposed to have advertising on the programme.

"And there are free-range eggs too!" squealed Davy. "Don't forget my hens."

The Whitby family were shuffled rather fast off camera.

Tony began to talk again. "But there is someone in this town who does not wish to see this marvellous piece of enterprise happen –

someone who has threatened to spoil it all – naming no names, of course."

The television then showed still photographs from the local paper of Thunderfoot guzzling kiwi fruit with obvious enjoyment. The name "Frescho" appeared in large letters on the lorry behind him.

"Because of their horse's unfortunate passion for exotic fruit, this family is faced with a stupendous fruit bill – a certain supermarket owner has threatened to take them to court

unless they pay immediately. I wonder why?''

What is he talking about? Mel wondered.

That evening, squashed into Sally's kitchen to watch the programme, they all found out.

This time Tony was speaking from the studio.

''Since we filmed this earlier, we have been doing a little research,'' he began. ''Lawsuits, as we all know, are very, very expensive –'' and here Tony paused. A look of intense excitement came upon his face. All of those watching realized it was the look of a journalist who is on to something. Possibly something big.

In Sally's kitchen everyone leaned forward in their seats.

''So why does a certain supermarket owner want to cause trouble for this particular family? I'll tell you.'' He spoke of the attempt made to stop the Whitbys by trying to find fault with the hygiene of the dairy.

''Permission could only be granted by the council. And who is the chairman of the council, folks? Mr Marshall Bullhead. And who is the owner of Freshco? One and the same – Mr Marshall Bullhead." Here Tony shook his head sadly. "All quite illegal: if our Bullhead friend stood to gain money from the failure of the Whitby and Family Dairy, he is not allowed to vote – let alone try to persuade the other councillors against the dairy." Then he switched to the story of Mr Fosset, and Bullhead's very nasty treatment of him. He also mentioned how Sally had been pestered to sell the railway field.

"And here's why –" he held up a wad of papers. "Plans: plans for an ultra new style Freshco Megastore on the site of the railway field and the dairy. Permission to be granted by . . . you've guessed it . . . the town council!"

Everyone in the kitchen gasped. Mrs Whitby turned to her husband. There were tears in her eyes as she said, "Sam, do you realize – it's all going to be all right: everything is going to be all right now."

Tony grinned. "I leave it to you, the viewer,

to decide – phone us to tell us what you think. Should Mr B get away with it? Do you want his megastore, or the Whitby and Family Dairy?

"So," he added, "it's my guess the Whitby family business is going to be very, very busy. If you want to order your daily pinta, you'd better be quick – I will be!"

The programme titles went out to film of Thunderfoot enjoying the contents of a box specially bought by the television company. It contained apples, melons, pawpaws and, of course, kiwi fruit.

"And he's still dribbling," said Angeline. "Yuk!"

Chapter 26

During the television programme, the switchboard was jammed – not only with supporters of the Whitby family, but with information and complaints about Bullhead. Nobody was surprised when he announced he was resigning as council chairman. (Nobody was much surprised when, a few months later, the Freshco supermarket closed, and another supermarket opened. Bullhead was not a name that appeared in the area after that.)

Sitting in the dairy office the following day, Mel said, "I wonder who told Tony all about Bullhead in the first place."

Mr Whitby grinned. "Guess," he said.

"I can't."

"It was Sally's old friend, Fearley."

"Fearley!" Mel gasped. "I was right then; there was a connection between them."

Dad nodded: "Originally, the two men had worked together. When they got into trouble for selling meat from diseased cattle, Bullhead got away scot-free. He made sure it was Fearley who got into trouble: that's why Fearley left in such a hurry. Now all this has come out, the police may feel they want to re-open the case."

"So this was Fearley's revenge," Mel said.

"Luckily for us, yes," said Dad.

Mrs Whitby smiled. "I could kiss that Tony."

"Don't you dare!" Dad told her.

"But look at all the orders we have now – and all due to that television programme." Mum turned on her computer and flicked through it to show the orders.

"Look!" Mel said. "Grindle and Grudge . . . one pint semi-skimmed and double cream on

Saturdays each – they said they wouldn't forget us."

Now everything was ready in the dairy, Mel and Dad spent every moment they could with Thunderfoot. First Mel walked him up and down the farm track with as many rattly old bottles as she could find. Then she took him on the roads, at first with Dad leading. She didn't go alone until she was absolutely sure he wasn't going to be frightened again. She even got Davy and Alice to help by making loud noises, shrieking and clashing saucepan lids. They enjoyed this enormously, and were very good at it. In the end you could have held a rock concert next to Thunderfoot and he wouldn't have minded.

At last Mel felt Thunderfoot was ready.

"Come and see." Paul Merrell took Mel by the hand. His eyes glittered with excitement. "It's finished."

The four students who had been working with him on the project also looked excited, but very tired too.

Mel followed them to the barn, which for so long she had been forbidden to enter. For some time now, the sawing and tapping sounds had ended, to be replaced by an even more intriguing silence. What could they have been doing in there?

Mr Merrell threw open the doors and the four students watched her face anxiously.

Mel gasped. It really was quite extraordinary. She had never seen anything like it. Larger than she had expected, it was intricately carved and painted. There were special cupboards for yoghurt and juices, and drawers to slide eggs into. On top was a sign that said "Whitby and Family Dairy". But on every flat surface available, were painted pictures. One showed a picture of cows grazing in a field, another was of the dairy house. There was a scene of hens in a farmyard, and baskets full of brown eggs.

Mr Merrell pointed. "See this one? Meg did that one."

"Oh, but it's Dad!" Mel exclaimed. Tall and gingery, with a milk crate in either hand, it was very definitely a portrait of Mr Whitby.

The student called Meg grinned sheepishly. "We all helped each other," she said. "Raf and Sandy built and carved it with Paul. Hamish and I painted it. It was a brilliant project."

"It's the most beautiful thing I have ever seen," Mel told them truthfully.

On the great day, everyone was up early. Mel had washed Thunderfoot the day before; today she and Bruno brushed him till he shone. It was hard to remember how thin and dull he had so recently been when you saw the glossy and muscular animal of today. His hooves gleamed with oil, and the feathery hairs above were snowy white. Sally showed Mel how to plait his long mane, and twine red ribbons through each plait. Mum and Davy had got together and made rosettes to decorate the bridle and harness. Even Angeline allowed that he "didn't look bad".

The milk had been delivered the previous evening and stored in the giant, walk-in fridges. Now Dad loaded it onto the beautiful float.

Mel had asked if she might go with him on the first day. Then of course Davy wanted to come, too. In the end, the whole family sat with Dad in the small cab. All along the way, children and their parents ran out to greet them. Old ladies smiled.

Thunderfoot arched his neck, and raised his hooves high. He loved all the attention, and all the children running round him. It was clear that he was going to enjoy his job, and was going to be very good at it.

Mr Whitby too was delighted to be back on the job. "And how much nicer to have Thunderfoot, instead of an electric milk float."

At last it was all over. Thunderfoot was safely fed and watered, and back in his field. The milk

crates were cleaned and ready for the next day. The hens were locked up for the night.

Mr Whitby sank down into a chair, suddenly very tired. He felt light with relief. He was aware, too, that it wasn't all going to be easy. They would have to make sure that the people on their books stayed there; and they would need quite a few more to make the business really pay for itself.

He knew that the next few months would be the testing time. He was tired now, and would be tired again. All sorts of things could still go wrong, but whatever happened he was going to do his best to keep off the dole queue again.

"Something else has come from all this," Dad said to Mel. "Some fancy interior designer asked who made the cart. He's desperate to get the four students to work for him when they finish college."

"That's wonderful," Mel said. So they would have jobs to go to at the end of their course.

She remembered being a member of the "clan" at school, and shuddered; it had been a near escape. Not everyone was so fortunate.

"It's all due to you, Mel," Dad said. "Without you, none of this would have happened."

Mel shook her head, thinking of the other girls in her class. "Luck," she said. "Luck and Mr Bullhead."

Mr Whitby leant back in his chair and sighed. "And now," he said, closing his eyes, "now I'd love a cup of tea."

Mel jumped up and put the kettle on. "I'll do it." She went over to the fridge. Suddenly she began to laugh. They all looked at her in surprise.

"What's the matter?" Dad said.

Mel held up the empty bottle. "Fine milkman you are," she said. "We've run out of milk!"